PUFFIN BOOKS

OWN GOAL

Tom Palmer is a football fan and author. He visits schools and libraries every week to talk about reading, writing and football.

It was reading about football that helped Tom to become a confident reader. He now has the job of his dreams: travelling the world to watch football matches, meeting players, then writing stories about them.

He lives in Yorkshire where he likes to be with his family, watch football and run.

You can find out more about Tom – and talk to him – through his website: *www.tompalmer.co.uk*

OWN GOAL

TOM PALMER

PUFFIN

PUFFIN BOOKS

Published by the Penguin Group
Penguin Books Ltd, 80 Strand, London WC2R ORL, England
Penguin Group (USA) Inc., 375 Hudson Street, New York, New York 10014, USA
Penguin Group (Canada), 90 Eglinton Avenue East, Suite 700, Toronto, Ontario, Canada M4P 2Y3
(a division of Pearson Penguin Canada Inc.)
Penguin Ireland, 25 St Stephen's Green, Dublin 2, Ireland (a division of Penguin Books Ltd)
Penguin Group (Australia), 250 Camberwell Road, Camberwell, Victoria 3124, Australia
(a division of Pearson Australia Group Pty Ltd)
Penguin Books India Pvt Ltd, 11 Community Centre, Panchsheel Park, New Delhi – 110 017, India
Penguin Group (NZ), 67 Apollo Drive, Rosedale, Auckland 0632, New Zealand
(a division of Pearson New Zealand Ltd)
Penguin Books (South Africa) (Pty) Ltd, 24 Sturdee Avenue, Rosebank,
Johannesburg 2196, South Africa

Penguin Books Ltd, Registered Offices: 80 Strand, London WC2R ORL, England

puffinbooks.com

First published 2011
001 – 10 9 8 7 6 5 4 3 2 1

Text copyright © Tom Palmer, 2011
All rights reserved

The moral right of the author has been asserted

Set in Sabon 12.5/17.25 pt
Typeset by Palimpsest Book Production Limited, Falkirk, Stirlingshire
Printed in Great Britain by Clays Ltd, St Ives plc

British Library Cataloguing in Publication Data
A CIP catalogue record for this book is available from the British Library

ISBN: 978-0-141-33119-5

www.greenpenguin.co.uk

MIX
Paper from
responsible sources
FSC www.fsc.org   FSC™ C018179

Penguin Books is committed to a sustainable
future for our business, our readers and our
planet. This book is made from paper certified
by the Forest Stewardship Council.

For my lovely sister, Sarah

CONTENTS

Monday

Tuesday

Wednesday

Part Two: Italy

Tuesday

Wednesday

Part Three: England

Thursday

Friday

PART ONE: ENGLAND

FRIDAY

GLORY SUPPORTER

'Who *are* you? Who *are* you?'

Danny was walking down the long corridor that ran the length of the main building at school when he heard it. The chanting of a football song. One he knew well.

But he carried on walking. Although he was the only person in the corridor that morning, there was no reason to think it was being aimed at him.

'WHO *ARE* YOU? WHO *ARE* YOU?' It came louder now.

Danny looked round this time to see three figures at the far end of the corridor. He knew who they were immediately. Theo Gibbs, from the sixth form. And his two mates, Andy and Ryan. Now what?

Ignore them?

Shout something back?

Just stand there, like he was now?

They wanted to get a reaction out of him: he knew that much.

A second chorus started up.

> LET'S ALL LAUGH AT CITY.
> LET'S ALL LAUGH AT CITY.
> NA NA NA-NA.
> HA!
> NA NA NA-NA.
> HA!

Danny wasn't surprised. He had been expecting this kind of thing to happen sooner.

Everyone at school knew he was a big City FC fan. He'd been a season-ticket holder long before City had become one of the best teams in Europe. And anyone who was a City fan was going to get stick this week.

When things like this happened you just had to walk away. That's what Dad would argue.

So Danny started to walk.

But he did not walk *away* from Theo and his cronies. He went *towards* them. And he knew exactly what he was going to say. That was because he knew exactly what *they* were going to say, even before they'd said it.

He stopped when he was a metre away from them.

'All right, City fan?' Theo said. He was medium height, thin, with black hair.

Danny gave a tight-lipped smile, but kept quiet. Situations like this were weird for him. Normally he would avoid arguments, both at home and here at school. He liked a quiet life and he was generally a very calm person, barely ever in trouble.

But when it came to City FC it was different. When it came to City FC it felt like it wasn't *him* who was being insulted. It was an insult to his football club and its thousands of supporters. That was why he was ready to stand his ground. That was what made this different.

Especially when the insult came from Theo Gibbs. Because Theo Gibbs supported the team Danny hated more than any other.

Forza FC of Italy.

'Looking forward to a beating on Wednesday?' Theo asked.

This was it. The reference to next week's match that he had been waiting for.

'Not a beating . . .' Danny said calmly.

'What? You think City can win against the best team in the world?' Theo sneered.

'I do,' Danny replied, glaring at the sixth-former.

Theo exploded with laughter.

But Danny still said nothing. He had done what he had wanted to do. Faced down Theo Gibbs. Kept calm. Done his duty to City. He turned and started to walk away. Even though he knew there was more to come.

'We are *so* going to take you apart,' Theo started again. 'Four or five–nil. We are better in every department. Our keeper. Our defenders. Our . . .'

As Theo went on, Danny reflected on the game next week.

City FC versus Forza FC in the Champions League semi-final. An English team versus an Italian team.

So why was it, then, that so many people supported Forza FC in this school? It was crazy. It did Danny's head in. But there was no escaping it. People were obsessed with Forza. Even Emily, Danny's sister, liked them. And she *hated* football. It was crazy enough when people here preferred to support the bigger English clubs, seeing as they had such a good team in their city. But to support a foreign team?

It didn't make sense.

'. . . and you know who is going to score the goals?' The sixth-former left his question hanging in the air, knowing it would vex Danny. 'You do know, don't you?'

Danny stood with his back to Theo. Now he *was* angry.

'Roberts. Your ex-player, Sam Roberts.' Danny could hear the smile in Theo's voice. 'Roberts knew which was the *best* team. And that's why he left City for Forza. Do you miss him?'

Inevitably, with the mention of his former favourite player, something snapped in Danny. He turned and marched back down the corridor towards Theo. Fast.

He noticed the sixth-former widen his feet. Like he was expecting a fight.

And Danny wondered. Could he? Would he? Should he . . . hit Theo Gibbs?

He breathed in and out. Deep and long. Just like he always did when he wanted to calm himself down – or, at least, stay in control.

And, when he reached the sixth-former, he stood right up in front of him and looked him directly in the eye.

'Will you be there?' Danny said calmly.

'What?' Theo's voice had weakened.

'I said, will *you* be there?'

Theo shrugged. 'No need.'

'Will you be *there*?' Danny insisted.

'I said, there's no need – I can watch it on TV.'

'Wearing your facsimile Forza shirt and drinking out of your facsimile Forza mug with your facsimile Forza blanket on your knee . . .' Danny said.

'No,' Theo said, stepping back very slightly, showing Danny he was rattled.

'No, *you* won't be there,' Danny said. 'But I will be. Like I am week after week after week because I am a proper football fan and *you* are a glory supporter.'

And, with that, Danny walked away, the corridor silent.

But it would not be his last clash with Theo Gibbs. Not by a long way. And the next encounter would be sooner than he expected.

SCHOOL PROJECT

Danny was pleased to see Charlotte already sitting in the classroom as he pushed through the door. And very pleased to see her look up at him and smile.

'What's up with you?' she asked, her dark eyes fixed on him.

Danny pushed a couple of chairs out of his path, slumped down in his seat and pulled a face.

'Theo Gibbs,' he said.

'What about him?'

'He's a . . .' Danny held back the word he had ready in his head to describe the sixth-former. 'You know.'

'He's all right,' Charlotte said.

Danny took a breath while trying to conceal his frown. *Charlotte* thought *Theo* was all right? Great. That just about topped it all off.

'Are you coming to the party tonight? At Cal's?'

Charlotte asked, not at all aware that she'd irritated Danny. 'Did he invite you?'

Danny shrugged. 'I don't know.' He felt insular, not really sure he *wanted* to go to a party. A night at home might suit him better, the mood he was in. There were bound to be more people at the party who called themselves Forza fans. It was like a disease had struck, some terrible virus. Hundreds of people, all supporting Forza, like Theo. And they'd be on his case. He knew that. He wanted to avoid them.

But he didn't want Charlotte to think he was boring, so he was relieved to see their media studies teacher, Mrs Page, come into the room and hear her raise her voice to start the class. He'd think about the party later.

'Today . . .' Mrs Page shouted, waiting for near silence. 'Today we are going to start our class work profiles that will count towards your final GCSE result.'

The volume in the room dropped to zero.

'As we discussed last week,' Mrs Page continued, 'each of you needs to choose a person to create a profile for. A living person. Someone you admire? Like Barack Obama, perhaps. Or an author you like to read: Stephenie Meyer, Roald Dahl, Jeff Kinney. Someone like that. Or we said it could be someone controversial. Someone you maybe *don't* like. Now you've had some time to think about it, I'd like to hear your ideas.'

Danny looked at Charlotte. 'Who are you doing?'

'Lady Gaga. What about you?'

'I dunno,' Danny said, shrugging.

Mrs Page picked on people in the room, asking them who they were going to profile.

'Jacqueline Wilson.'

'Robert Pattinson.'

'Katie Price.'

Danny barely listened to the names his classmates suggested. He was too busy thinking about Theo. And Charlotte. And Forza FC. And how it made him *sick* so many people supported them. He could feel an anger building in him. Anger towards Forza FC. Towards their owner, Salvatore Fo. Towards their fans. And he knew why: he felt vulnerable. If City lost to Forza, he'd never hear the last of it. From dozens of people.

His classmates were still reeling off their heroes.

'Kurt Cobain.'

'Jeremy Clarkson.'

'SpongeBob SquarePants.'

The class exploded with laughter. Danny didn't join in. He was deep inside himself now.

'Danny Harte. Who are you choosing?'

Mrs Page had selected him seeing that he was not concentrating on what he should be, pouncing like a predator.

And Danny, without thinking – remembering Mrs Page's remark *Someone you maybe* don't *like* – had decided.

'Salvatore Fo,' he said. 'The owner of Forza FC.'

The more Danny thought about it, as he walked home from school, the more he wanted to get started on this new school project. He was going to find out about Forza FC's owner. The bad stuff. And he would put it all in his profile and then online, so *everyone* could read it.

All the little pieces of information he knew about Fo were coming together in his head.

He already knew Fo was dodgy. Seriously dodgy. Danny had read about it in *World Soccer* magazine and on the Internet. Fo had Mafia connections. There had been several court cases for corruption and stuff to do with bribery. And he went out with women young enough to be his granddaughters.

This was actually going to be fun. Now that Danny had an outlet for his rage, he knew he was going to be all right. Now he had a mission. And that mission was to show everyone at his school and everywhere else what a dodgy man Salvatore Fo was. And to stop so many people supporting Forza FC.

At home, Danny opened the front door and sprinted upstairs so he could get his thoughts about the school project into his notebook before he forgot them. He didn't say anything to his parents, who were talking in the kitchen with the door closed.

Danny went into his bedroom. A large desk dominated the room. And back on the wall there was a huge notice board with maps and lists and pictures pinned to it. This room was more than a bedroom to Danny. *This* was his nerve centre. The place where he recorded crimes and tried to solve them.

Because, as well as football, Danny Harte had another passion: detection. Trying to get to the bottom of thefts, disappearances and murders consumed his life.

In the last year he had solved a string of crimes related to football. He hadn't done it all on his own. Charlotte had helped. A lot. But his main partner – in crime *solving* – was his friend, a football journalist on the local newspaper, Anton Holt.

Holt had access to players, to information, to City FC. And now – bizarrely – Holt was going out with Danny's sister. But that was another story.

As he sat down at the desk and started making his notes about Salvatore Fo, Danny heard his parents' voices through the floorboards. Voices that were getting louder. Much louder. It was *not* a normal discussion. In fact, there were few normal discussions in the house these days. *Everything* seemed to end in an argument.

He couldn't make out the words. But he could tell that his parents were both angry.

Danny put his pen down, opened his bedroom door and stood at the top of the stairs. He wanted to hear them more clearly.

'So what are you going to do?' his dad's voice asked.

'I've told you.' That was his mum.

'Not yet. You have to wait.'

'I know I have to wait. But I'm sick of waiting. Sick to death.' His mum's voice was getting louder again.

'Just until the summer. We can all cope with it better then. After Emily's A-levels and Danny's exams.'

Danny had absolutely no idea what was going on. But it didn't sound good.

And then he heard his mum scream, 'I can't wait until the summer! I am cracking up. I have to get out. Out!'

Her voice was so hard, so shrill, that Danny didn't register to himself that he had walked down the stairs, along the hall and had pushed the kitchen door open.

He stood facing his parents.

He had nothing to say. He wasn't even thinking.

Silence followed. An empty, useless, pathetic, stupid silence.

Danny looked into the kitchen.

His mother was just standing there staring at him, tears running down her cheeks. Danny was struck again by how different she was these days. She had been going to the gym, losing weight, learning Italian. And she *looked* different.

She didn't speak.

Dad was sitting on a stool, his face pointing towards the ceiling. He often did that. He was blind. But he still knew his son had just come into the room.

'Danny?' Dad asked.

'Yeah,' Danny replied. 'It's me.'

Still his mum said nothing. She had moved to the other side of the kitchen and now was sat at the table, her head in her hands.

Danny watched Dad stand and follow her, to put his hand on Mum's shoulder. Then he saw his mother move her shoulder away.

That said it all. It gave Danny the answer to the question forming in his mind.

But he had to know. He had to hear it from them.

'What's happening?' he asked.

Neither of his parents answered.

Danny could hear a car accelerating outside the house. And someone calling a dog.

'Tell me,' he insisted. Because he knew exactly what they would tell him. He just didn't know whether they had the nerve to do it.

'They're splitting up.'

The voice came from behind him.

His sister's voice.

'No, you're not,' Danny said, keeping his eyes on his mum and dad.

But neither of them denied it.

PARTY

An hour later, there was a knock at Danny's bedroom door. It was his dad.

'Can I come in?'

'Hang on a minute,' Danny answered. He was changing his clothes, about to go out to the party. Cal *had* invited him. And there was no way he wanted to stay at home tonight.

Once he was dressed, Danny opened the door.

'Can we talk?' Dad asked.

'I'm off to a party,' Danny said.

Dad nodded.

Danny tolerated the silence between them for as long as he could, then said, 'Can we talk about it tomorrow? I just want to get my head round stuff.'

His dad nodded again. 'OK,' he said. 'Whenever you're ready. Do you want a lift from your mum?'

'No thanks,' Danny said. 'I need to be alone. You know.'

'I think so,' Dad said, standing out of the way to let Danny walk down the stairs.

It was cold outside. And as Danny ran – because he felt like running – he enjoyed the chill of the air on his skin. He didn't really want to get his head round anything. He didn't really want to think about his mum and dad at all. He wanted to escape from his thoughts altogether, thoughts that were starting to make his head hurt.

He turned left at the end of his street and ran down towards the park. As he ran, he counted car and window stickers. This was a variation on a game he played when he wanted to not think about something. City versus Forza stickers. How many of each? If there were more City, then City would win the game next week.

But there weren't more City stickers: there were more supporting *Forza*. Way more.

Danny stopped counting and ran down the centre of the road, his eyes fixed on the woods in the park ahead. Birds were wheeling over them, their dark silhouettes against the sky turning and turning again.

He didn't really want to think about Forza FC, but it was better than thinking about home.

Why was it that thousands of people in this city – and cities across the world – supported Forza? This was the question that came back to him again and again. It had to be more than the fact that Sam Roberts, England's top footballer, played for them. People liked Real Madrid when David Beckham was there. But only a bit. They'd not become sticker-sticking, shirt-buying idiots like this Forza FC lot.

It made Danny angry. And the more angry it got him, the better he felt.

He ran through the park, beside the lake, up the slope and past the bandstand where he saw a couple sitting together in the dark.

After the park, Danny slowed to a walk. He didn't want to arrive at the party with a pink face and sweating. But a part of him wished he could have carried on running up into the hills on the edge of the city.

The party sounded quiet when Danny arrived.

The front door was wide open. The house was big and built of dark stone. Danny noticed the two houses on each side had Forza stickers or flags in the windows. Cal's house didn't. That was a relief, at least.

As Danny edged inside he heard a boy's voice complaining that Cal didn't have MTV. 'What are we supposed to watch?'

It was a voice that was familiar. Too familiar.

'We don't have Sky,' Cal said.

'What? Everyone has Sky!'

Danny heard a laugh. A girl's. Familiar again.

'*We* don't,' Cal repeated.

'Why not?'

'There's a music system. That'll have to do.' Cal was now sounding irritated.

Danny chose this moment to walk into the room.

And there they were.

Cal, the host.

Charlotte, with her friends Molly and Beth.

And Theo Gibbs, with another boy who Danny didn't recognize.

The room was lit by three lamps. There were drinks on the table at the side of the room, and a pile of bags of crisps.

'Danny!' Theo shouted. 'How's it going?'

Danny said nothing. He didn't even catch Theo's eye.

'You're not still angry about what I said about City, are you?' Theo asked, then turned to laugh with his friend.

Danny said hello to Cal. Then he looked at

Charlotte in a way that he hoped would say *please come and talk to me* without drawing attention to himself.

It worked. Charlotte came straight over. Just as four more people from school walked into the house, distracting the others.

Theo started retelling their clash at school. But Danny would not rise to it. He would just ignore anything and everything that Theo said. He knew that, deep down, most people would think Theo was an idiot.

Danny looked into Charlotte's eyes. He knew *his* eyes looked sad.

'What is it?' she asked urgently. 'What's happened?'

This was what Danny liked about Charlotte. She knew when he wanted to talk. She knew when things were serious, without him needing to say a word. She could almost read his mind. It reminded him a bit of how he was with his dad. Except he felt very differently about Charlotte.

He turned his back to the rest of the room and spoke in a low voice. He felt a tension building in his arms and across his shoulders because of what he had to say. But he wanted to say it, wanted to tell her.

'My mum and dad are splitting up,' he said. But

that was all he *could* say. This was the first time he'd put it into words. And, for some reason, saying it aloud made him feel like he had been hit by a train.

However much Danny liked being with Charlotte, he was not happy at the party. He had thought coming out would be better than sitting in his room. But it wasn't. Too many people were irritating him. Theo. A couple of lads who were drinking cider. Everyone.

Danny just stood there, in a circle with Charlotte and her friends, listening to other people talking, but saying nothing. He made the odd facial gesture: a look of shock when someone said something shocking, a smile when someone said something funny. But he was not moved by anything.

And he had this pain inside his stomach. Or was it in his head? He wasn't sure. But it felt bad. And he knew he had to get out of there.

He put his hand on Charlotte's shoulder. She looked up at him.

'I'm off,' he said.

'OK,' she nodded. 'I'll come.'

But Danny shook his head. 'I'm best going on my own. I feel . . . I just want to go home.'

He saw Charlotte try to smile, but she looked worried.

'See you,' he said, taking his hand off her shoulder. Then he walked out into the night.

SATURDAY

GOING AWAY

Danny woke at six thirty the next morning.

No one else was awake.

It took him seconds to make up his mind.

There was no way he could face today. Everyone would be at home. And probably wanting to *talk* about things. Talk, talk, talk! He didn't want to talk. That was the last thing he wanted to do.

His mind drifted to City FC. They were playing away today. In London, against Tottenham. He wished they were at home.

Home games meant being nervous all day, gathering with thousands of others, singing, shouting, the day consumed by football.

If *only* he was allowed to go to away games . . .

The next thought took Danny completely by surprise.

He *would* go.

That was it.

His parents weren't allowed to split up, but they *were*. So why couldn't he go to an away match?

Immediately his body was fizzing with excitement.

Now he had to get out of the house as quickly as possible. Before anyone else woke up.

Danny threw on some clothes, including his City FC top under a hoody. Then he grabbed the City piggy bank that he used to save up for his season ticket. He had £115 in there. He took the lot. He'd worry about next season next season.

Downstairs, he decided to go without breakfast. He didn't want to risk waking anyone by clinking cutlery and crockery. He could get something in town.

He left a note on the telephone table. *Gone to Charlotte's for the day. I'm OK. See you tonight. Danny.*

All he needed now was the house keys. They were usually in the front room somewhere.

Danny was already searching about in the dark before he realized someone else was in the room with him. He stopped and backed up to the door. As his eyes adjusted, he saw who it was.

Dad.

Sleeping on the sofa.

Danny felt a great lunge in his stomach. And his eyes filled with tears. It was the sight of his dad alone, sleeping on the sofa, like some husband from *EastEnders* who had been kicked out of his wife's bed. He thought of his mum upstairs, alone as well.

It struck him hard. Every night, since he'd been born, his mum and dad had slept next to each other in the big bed. He'd slept in there with them when he was very little, if he was scared or ill. But now this . . .

And it seemed so pointless. So stupid.

Part of him felt like waking them both up and shouting at them. They were idiots.

So, to contain his feelings, he quickly found the keys, left the room, let himself out of the front door and walked, head down, to the end of the street, turning left towards the bus stops into town.

The city centre was quiet. Not many cars. Mostly buses filled with people in shop uniforms going to work. And one guy with a large blue bag – marked *igoal* – slung over his shoulder.

But there *were* several groups of men.

All in dark clothes. All clutching plastic bags full of cans or bottles.

Danny stood for a while in City Square watching them.

One group of younger men were shouting and laughing. After a while a large van pulled up, the door slid open and they all piled in. More shouting. More laughing. Then the slam of the sliding door, the revving of the engine and the silence after it had gone.

Danny saw two older men heading into the station. They had City shirts on, so he followed them. At the ticket office they asked for day returns with a London Underground travelcard. Danny copied them when it was his turn. Then he followed them to buy a newspaper in WHSmith.

The station was filled with the murmur of mostly male voices. It felt a bit like a church before a service. There were a lot of people travelling to see football. But not just City fans. There was a couple in Leeds United tops and another man wearing a Celtic scarf. Everyone seemed to be going to a match.

And Danny was one of them. A travelling fan. It felt good. And he knew he would remember this day for the rest of his life.

He followed the men through the barriers to platform eight and read the screen: 08:05 to London. The train was one of those long dark-coloured ones that he'd seen sometimes from his mum's car as they went speeding through the countryside.

Danny climbed on to the train and sat in a carriage near the two men in City shirts he'd been following. A minute later four other men got on. All were clearly City fans. In fact Danny was pretty sure he'd seen them at the football before. One of them winked at him, as he walked by.

Then the doors closed and the train eased away from the platform.

Danny thrilled with excitement again.

He'd got up early and come into town.

He'd bought his ticket.

He'd gone to the platform.

He was on a train with some other City fans.

And now the train was moving out of the station.

This was it. No turning back.

Danny was, for the first time, going to watch City away on his own.

UNDERGROUND

Danny knew he was in London when the train started to slow down and he saw Arsenal's Emirates stadium through the windows on the left. It was an amazing building, like a massive spaceship. There were banners all around it, featuring great players from Arsenal's past. Danny took a photo of it with his iPhone, a recent birthday present. He wondered if Spurs' ground would look as impressive.

He noticed that the group of four men he was planning to follow were getting ready. He tried to avoid being seen by them. He didn't want them to know he was following them, but he understood that the easiest way of getting to the Spurs stadium was to stay close to them.

The train passed through a couple of dark tunnels, then into King's Cross station.

When it stopped, Danny's heart started thudding.

He could feel the fast pulse in his throat as he followed the men off the train.

This was a bit like the detective work he had done before. Tracking people without being seen. He had spied on England players and dangerous burglars this way. He figured that following a group of middle-aged football fans wouldn't be so hard compared to that.

Except it was. Really hard. The station was packed with thousands of people who all seemed to have lost their manners. People shoved into Danny and he found it hard to keep up with the men. If he lost them, he'd be in trouble.

But each time he thought they had disappeared, the men suddenly appeared nearby. Like they were waiting for someone *they'd* lost. And once they were out of the station, there were fewer people around, so it was easier to track them.

The men headed down a staircase, marked Underground. Danny had been on the London Underground before, with his mum and dad. He understood how it worked. So he let the men stand away from him on the platform, knowing he'd be able to pick them up again once they arrived at what he thought was the right tube station: Seven Sisters.

The name made him smile. Seven sisters! He had trouble coping with one.

He looked at his watch. 11:30.

And, for the first time since he'd left the house that morning, his mind went back there.

Mum and Dad.

Emily.

He knew they wouldn't be worried about him. He was independent. He regularly went off for the day. And they would have called or texted him if they *had* been worried.

Danny checked his iPhone to see if he'd missed a message. He hadn't.

He wondered what it would be like at home.

Emily would have gone out with her friends. Shopping.

He thought back to his dad sleeping on the sofa. Maybe he would be there still, probably listening to Radio 5. And he thought of his mum. At her laptop, working. Always working. He wondered which one of them would feel the loneliest.

The noise of chanting broke into his thoughts.

> *City till I die*
> *I'll be City till I die*
> *I know I am*
> *I'm sure I am*
> *I'm City till I die.*

The train had stopped, the doors were open and hundreds of men were getting off. City fans, their deep voices filling the narrow tunnels and staircases that led up to the surface. Danny noticed other people standing aside, nervously letting them pass. Families. Couples. Old people.

But there was no hint of trouble. The City fans were behaving well, one even helping a woman carry her push-chair up a flight of stairs.

Amid this mass of City fans, Danny felt good. All his worries about his mum and dad seemed to melt away when he was in the crowd, chanting and laughing. Even though he was on his own, he did not *feel* like he was alone. Now he had taken his hoody off, other City fans turned and talked to him. Asking if he'd heard the team news. Making jokes about London being busy.

And Danny felt free.

Now all he needed was a ticket to the match.

He walked up a long wide road from the tube station, City and Spurs fans intermingling. Lots of shouting and laughing. The fans of two teams talking without a hint of trouble.

And outside the stadium, it was equally amazing. Strong smells of hot dogs and fried onions. People stopping to buy flags and badges and T-shirts.

Danny spotted one man, selling something. Shiftily looking around him every few seconds.

A ticket tout. Danny had no doubt.

He stood nearby and listened.

'Main stand, forty quid. City stand, fifty.'

Danny frowned. Fifty pounds? He'd already spent thirty on the train. But he knew he'd be lucky to get one cheaper. It was an adult ticket. The tout would not be offering children's discounts.

He walked up to the man.

'Can I have one in the City end, please?'

The tout grinned. He had massive arms and a heavy stubble.

'Sixty quid, son.'

'You just said fifty,' Danny said, stepping backwards.

The man laughed. 'OK. Fifty quid.'

Danny *sort of* liked the man. He knew what he was doing wasn't legal. But he seemed OK, even though he'd tried to cheat him.

'Can I have a young person's discount, please?' Danny asked, keeping his face straight.

The man doubled over, laughing again. Then he called to another man standing about ten metres away. 'We've got a good one here. Kids' discount he wants.'

Danny pulled five ten-pound notes out of his

pocket. He knew he was stupid spending almost half of his season ticket money for next year on one game, but this was a big day. This was his first away game on his own.

The tout took his money and handed him a ticket.

'Go round that way, son,' he said, pointing. Then he peeled a ten-pound note off the money Danny had given him and handed it back. 'Kids' discount.'

Danny stood near the gates to the away stand, still clutching his ticket. There was over an hour to kick-off and he wanted to see what was going on. He loved watching football crowds.

Some City fans were gathering. Danny could see they all had matching T-shirts on. But not City shirts. In fact, each T-shirt had a letter on it.

And Danny knew who these fans were. Protesters.

City FC were involved in an ownership battle. Some very rich foreigners wanted to buy the club. A lot of the fans were unhappy, worried that City would go the way of other teams who had been bought out, then got into financial trouble.

Danny could see the police to the right of the protesters.

The atmosphere had changed. The excitement of the crowds coming out of the tube station and the sense of fun had passed. And Danny couldn't work out why. But it had definitely changed.

He stayed well back from the protesters. That was how he noticed another group of City fans. The protesters were mainly older men, about the age of Danny's dad. But the new group were younger, mostly. They had shaven heads and big arms, like the ticket tout. Some of them, anyway. They were chanting something. But nothing Danny had heard before. And that was when he realized that they weren't City fans at all.

Danny glanced at the police.

Had they seen this?

He knew what was happening. He had read about it. Protests by normal fans were often infiltrated by troublemakers. People who just wanted a fight.

Now Danny was convinced that something very bad was about to happen.

TROUBLE

Danny watched the new group of men moving slowly towards the back of the gathered protesters. He was also keeping an eye out for the police. Had they seen what was about to happen? Was Danny right that this was going to end in trouble?

He couldn't be sure.

What he *did* know was that this was not like the normal protests he'd seen over the last few weeks.

Since Sir Richard Gawthorpe had lost control at City FC – thanks to Danny – the club had been up for sale. Several foreign investors had tried to buy it. And some of them were the kind of people who took over a business or a sports team and sold parts of it off to make money. A group of fans wanted to stop this happening, by trying to raise the money to buy it themselves. These protesters were part of that group. Peaceful protesters trying to make their point.

But Danny could feel deep down in his stomach that this protest was not going to be peaceful. And his dad came to mind. *Go with your gut reaction*, he would say. *Sometimes there is no time to think.*

So Danny did what his dad would tell him to. If he could stop something bad happening, he should. He wanted to be a detective in the police force, didn't he? And that was the point of being in the police: stopping bad things happening.

Danny walked over to the police he had seen nearby. Just as the protesters were starting to wave their banners and chant their chant, peacefully and without violence. And just as the other men were moving ever closer to the genuine protesters.

Danny found a policeman who was standing at the edge of the crowd.

'Excuse me?'

'Yes, son?'

'There's a group of men infiltrating the protesters. I know the protesters. They're City fans. But I've never seen the other men.'

The policeman smiled, but something in his eyes suggested he thought Danny was just a silly boy. He glanced over to the crowd when he heard the noise of the protest growing. That was when his face changed.

He nodded. His voice was different now. 'That's

because they're a well-known hooligan gang, son. Well spotted.'

Then the policeman was on his radio. He gabbled something into it and – almost immediately – there was the sound of engines roaring. Danny had heard this before: police vans being driven fast in low gears. A sound familiar to football fans around the world.

They came from two directions, catching the fans by surprise. And, for a moment, everyone froze.

Danny stood back against the wall of the stadium and watched the small side street being invaded by uniformed police.

He also watched the new group of men. He wanted to see what they would do.

Would they fight – or run?

Danny's question was answered quickly.

The troublemakers were running, having clearly given up their plan to disrupt the protest. The protesters – the genuine City fans – were standing still, not doing anything. Not wanting to cause trouble. Danny noticed the older men he'd been following from the train among them.

He saw several of the troublemakers escape. There were back streets and alleyways everywhere. But the police caught some of them.

It wasn't what Danny could *see* that shocked him. It was what he could *hear*. Banging on the side of the police van. Police horse's hooves on the tarmac. Shouting, from both the fans and the police.

It was chaos.

But, because he knew he was safe standing up against the stadium, away from the trouble, Danny felt more excited than scared.

Eventually the clamour died down. Other fans had started to arrive. More normal noises, like the boom of the announcer inside the stadium, returned.

Now that the police had dealt with the hooligans, the officer Danny had spoken to came over. He was breathing heavily. Danny had seen him bundle at least three hooligans into a police van. He would be shattered.

'Like I said, son,' he breathed again, 'that was well spotted. Thank you.'

Compared to the excitement outside the stadium, the game itself was dull.

0–0 at full time.

The best bit had been the protesters, lining up with their T-shirts spelling out KEEP CITY IN CITY.

Both teams had seemed nervous about committing players forward. Showing each other too much respect. Danny wondered if the managers had made an agreement that a draw would be an acceptable result.

But that was typical Danny. Always looking for conspiracy in football. Some new match-fixing scandal.

Danny reflected on all this later, as his train headed north. Passing the Emirates stadium again. This time Arsenal's home ground was surrounded by people, mostly wearing red. Arsenal had a five thirty kick-off. Their chance to go top of the league.

Danny walked through the train to try to find the men he had been sat near earlier and had seen at the football, lined up with the protesters. He wanted to hear what they had to say about the day. Not so much the game, but the trouble before it.

And there they were, next to the buffet car. Each with a can of beer in front of them.

First they talked about the game. Then, inevitably, the trouble.

'We were lucky the coppers came in when they did. That group of thugs were about to make it kick off.'

'I know. Something like that could ruin it for us.'

'Dead lucky. Those police came in and helped just in time.'

The four men raised their glasses and toasted the police.

Danny knew what they meant about things being ruined. If there *had* been trouble, the protesters, who were always peaceful, would have been blamed. He felt good that he'd been able to help.

'Anyway, let's talk about the meeting,' one of the men said.

Danny sat up, but tried not to look over. What was this? What meeting?

'Right. Monday night. In the Playhouse Theatre. It seats two hundred. We've got a couple of journalists coming – and hopefully an ex-player.'

'Not Sir Richard Gawthorpe, then?' one of the men cut in.

The four men laughed.

'Back from the dead.'

Danny felt a chill at the mention of that name. Sir Richard Gawthorpe. The first man he had taken on in his role as football detective. Gawthorpe had been chairman of the club then. He'd kidnapped his own player – Sam Roberts –

44

and tried to make money out of it by selling shirts with Roberts on the back.

It was Danny who had stopped him.

'He's long dead,' one of the men said. 'You don't need to worry about him.'

Suddenly another voice broke in. A woman further along the carriage.

'This meeting? Can anyone come?'

'Definitely, love. Bring anyone you can.'

'Is it for fans? People who want to join the protest movement?'

'It is.'

'What time?'

'Seven p.m. The Playhouse Theatre, in the city centre.'

'I'll be there,' the woman said.

And so will I, Danny thought, smiling. Then wondered if his mum and dad would let him.

They would. He knew it.

And then he felt a shock run through him. Mum and Dad. What with all the excitement of the day, he had barely thought about them for hours. He was amazed. And actually quite pleased.

But now, as the train headed north towards home, he began to feel bad again. And, for the first time, an unwelcome thought crept into his head.

All of this stuff he'd been involved in, trying to solve crimes. It had caused a lot of trouble at home.

For instance, he'd invaded a football pitch with his dad's permission. His mum went mad with his dad for that.

He'd also been shot at several times, been chased round Moscow by a private army, been caught and taken to a cellar to be executed but had got away. And he'd told his dad about all this, but not his mum. His mum kind of knew there were secrets he'd told Dad but not her.

And, worst of all, he'd been arrested and Mum and Dad had come to pick him up and his mum had made his dad tell him to give up his detective work, even though he knew his dad didn't want him to.

He thought about all the occasions his mum and dad had wanted different things from him. It was bound to cause tension.

Maybe, he thought, it was because of him that his parents were splitting up.

SUNDAY

SUNDAY LUNCH

It was Sunday. And Sunday meant Sunday lunch.

The meal that Mum insisted they always have together.

Everyone had to be there.

No one could go out.

No excuses.

They'd have a roast of some sort, with all the veg and some gravy. Plus a fancy pudding, like a fruit pie, usually with custard.

Dad started the preparations at about eleven in the morning, as usual. Peeling the vegetables, putting the meat in the oven. That meant it was definitely going to happen. Even today. And, once someone had started, no one would dare to stop it.

So Danny went into the kitchen and offered to help. Dad asked him to set the table. Nobody had quizzed him about the day before.

This was the only time they ever *set* a table. In

the posh dining room, used only on Sundays and at Christmas. The fancy cutlery had to be laid out, along with napkins. And the best glasses. And various other things they had always done.

This was their family ritual. One of the things that bound them together.

But Danny found it weird today. All the things that were so normal seemed suddenly so pointless.

As he was setting the table, Emily came in. She shut the door behind her.

'Are you OK?' she asked.

Danny shrugged. 'I suppose so.'

He watched his sister fidgeting, wanting to say something.

'I'm worried about you,' she said.

'I'm fine,' Danny answered. Then he thought about her. 'What about you?'

Emily lowered her voice. 'I have to tell you something.' There was a tone in her voice that was out of place with the gloom of the house. Something like excitement.

Danny straightened a fork on the table and turned to face his sister.

'What is it?'

'What?'

'What do you want to tell me?'

'I'm –'

Her words were interrupted by a crash, then louder voices coming from the kitchen. Danny and Emily stared at each other as they listened.

It was Mum first. 'Oh no . . . the gravy jug . . .'

Dad's voice next. 'I'm sorry, love. I was rinsing it and . . .'

'I loved that jug. You're so clumsy!'

No reply from Dad.

'I loved that jug,' Mum repeated.

'I'm sorry. I'll buy a new one.'

'They don't do them any more. It was from 1992. It was a wedding present from my uncle . . .'

No reply again.

Danny wanted to go in and defend his dad. Speak on his behalf. He ran through his mind what he might say. And he realized he'd only end up defending his mum from the things his *dad* might say.

It had gone quiet in the kitchen, like Mum and Dad knew Danny and Emily were listening.

'They're whispering now,' Emily said. 'I'll tell you. About that thing. I –'

But just as she was about to say whatever she was going to say for the second time, Mum came in.

For a moment she just stood there. Then she spoke.

'What can I do?' she asked.

At first Danny and Emily did not say anything. Danny wondered if his mum had ever asked him a question like this. Like she wanted *them* to tell *her* what to do. She was always the one doing the telling.

But he knew that he should give her a job. She'd asked. It was something she wanted.

'The napkins?' Danny suggested.

Mum nodded gratefully and walked across to the cupboard where they were kept.

Danny felt his sister's hand on his back, then saw her pass out of the room. That was something else strange. A gesture of affection like that from Emily. He wasn't sure if that had happened before either.

But the moment was gone. Whatever his sister was going to tell him, it had passed. It would come out sometime soon. Danny knew *that* well enough.

Sunday lunch was eaten in silence. All four of them had made some attempt to ask a question that would start a conversation. But all four had failed.

Danny wondered if he should tell them about the day before, and the trouble at the football. At least that would get his mum going.

He decided not to.

So, for most of the meal, he listened to the clink of knives and forks on plates, so loud in the gloomy silence it could have been a sword fight.

Minute by minute the tension rose.

For the first time, Sunday lunch was not about family *togetherness*. It was about the opposite.

Danny could barely swallow for thinking that this could be the last time they did this.

And then Emily broke the silence. A sudden sentence. Her big secret spilling out.

'I'm moving in with Anton,' she said.

For Danny the next couple of seconds was like the moment at a match when the ball is struck and, although everyone knows it is going to hit the net, they do not react.

A pause. An intake of breath.

'WHAT?' Mum was standing up, her napkin on the floor.

'I'm moving out. I'm going to live with Anton.'

'NO!' Mum was shaking her head. She looked at Dad.

His face did not alter.

'No,' Mum said again.

'I'm going, Mum. I'll be eighteen soon enough. I can.'

Danny looked out of the window. So, his sister was going. Going to live with Anton. In the sky outside, there were two planes thirty thousand feet up. Crossing each other's paths, their vapour trails making a cross in the sky. Danny watched. When he looked back into the room his sister was not there any more and his dad was clearing the table.

Then he started to have that feeling growing inside him again. Like he had been hit by a truck.

'Danny, I need to talk to your dad,' Mum said.

'OK,' Danny replied, in as normal a voice as he could muster. 'I need to do my homework, anyway.'

In his room, Danny turned his laptop on. It was time to do his homework. His family could go on being his family and doing what they wanted. But he had a job to do. He felt calm.

That's what he told himself.

That's what he *had* to tell himself.

He put his headphones on and started to type into Google.

He entered 'Fo + crime'.

There were 7,789,023 entries.

Fo has been accused of links to the Mafia . . .

Salvatore Fo's close friends have been found guilty of numerous crimes . . .

Fo's manipulation of the Italian media is a crime . . .

Fo in bid to emulate Mussolini, the Italian dictator of the 1930s and . . .

Suddenly Danny felt anger. A rage boiling inside him.

He looked up Mussolini on Wikipedia. He was the man who ran Italy in the 1930s and '40s. A big bald man who liked shouting a lot. Someone who wanted to control everyone and would do whatever it took to achieve that. Like Hitler in Germany.

Danny was going to do a good job with this project. He was going to make the owner of Forza FC look like a monster.

He was going to do it, because he felt like it. And because he hated Forza. And because he hated Theo Gibbs. And because it was better than thinking about his mum and his dad and Emily and Anton and the burning feeling that it was his fault that his parents were splitting up.

MONDAY

THEO AND CHARLOTTE

'Morning, Danny.'

Danny came down for breakfast the next day wondering if, like Saturday, anybody would be there.

Today there was just Dad.

He'd heard his mum go out first thing. And Emily had left the night before.

'Tea?' Dad asked.

'Yes please,' Danny said.

Dad reached for two mugs and put them on the counter.

Danny and his dad were comfortable with silences. They never talked just to fill them. Silences were just silences. But not today. Today there was a massive unfilled chasm there too.

Danny decided to fill it.

'How are you feeling?' he asked.

He watched his dad smile as he poured water on to tea bags.

'I'm OK, Danny,' Dad answered in a weary voice. 'But what about *you*?'

'I feel sad,' Danny said, trying to be as honest as he could. 'But I don't know exactly what I feel.'

'I'm sorry this is happening now,' Dad said, after pausing. 'Before your exams.'

'I'm sorry it's happening at all,' Danny replied, without thinking.

He watched his dad's shoulders slump, then firm up again.

'This has been going on for a while, Danny. Your mum and I have not been getting on, not been happy.'

'I know,' Danny said.

Mum and Dad had been on a holiday together recently. Trying to work things out. Danny knew that was why they'd gone without him. They'd been arguing a lot too. Often about him.

And that was *still* going round his mind. That he was to blame for this.

The time when he'd been arrested.

The time he'd been involved in solving the kidnap of Sam Roberts.

The time when his dad had let him run on to the pitch at the football.

Danny realized that a lot of his parents' arguments had been about him.

But he wouldn't let the next thought come into his mind. The thought that he was to blame kept coming up, over and over. A thought he couldn't face.

'There's a meeting at the Playhouse Theatre tonight,' he said to Dad, interrupting his own thoughts. 'About the City takeover.'

'Right,' Dad said. 'How, er . . . how did you find out about that?'

Danny immediately thought he should lie. Make up some story about where he'd heard it. Not on the train back from City's away game on Saturday.

But why should he bother lying?

What was the point? What difference would it make in the end?

And he knew his dad hated lies.

'I went to Spurs on Saturday,' Danny confessed. 'I overheard some men talking about it.'

Dad said nothing.

'Do you want to come?' Danny asked.

'To the next away game?' Dad said, with a half-laugh.

Danny wanted to laugh himself, but found he couldn't. 'To the meeting.'

'Yes please.'

'OK,' Danny said.

'Danny?'

'Yeah.'

'Seeing as we're being honest . . . I sort of knew you were heading off to the Spurs game, so I, er . . . I phoned a couple of guys I know who were going down on the train. Asked them to look out for you.'

Danny walked across the park to school, wondering about what his dad had done. Those men on the train. The one who had winked. Were they his dad's friends? He thought he'd been following *them*, being all clever like a detective, but, in fact, they'd been waiting for him, making it easy for him. No wonder he'd found it so straightforward.

He didn't know whether to feel angry or pleased. So he just walked through the quiet park, without feeling either.

Danny didn't notice the silver car tracking him as he made his way across fields and roads. Or the determined face of the man behind the wheel.

School was a contrast to the peace of the park. The corridors were packed with hundreds of children and with teachers shouting orders.

It was chaotic and noisy and overheated and people kept barging into him.

Danny felt like walking out.

Why not?

He had a good excuse. His parents were splitting up. He was feeling depressed. He could say that. No problem. Just go to see his head of year and tell the truth. Maybe they'd order a taxi to take him home. Give him the week off, even.

But Danny *did* want to see Charlotte.

And he knew that, if he took the day off, his parents would hear about it and there'd be more recriminations at home. More arguments. More reasons for his mum and dad to split up.

So he headed down the corridor, dodging bags and running year-sevens, hoping to get to the classroom before registration.

But just as he made it to the door, a familiar form came out of the room.

Someone who should not have been in there.

Theo Gibbs.

'All right, Danny,' Theo said, deadpan.

Danny smiled. 'Fine, thanks. You?'

'Fine, mate.' Theo lowered his voice, so he was almost whispering. 'You missed a great party at the weekend.'

Danny smiled again, expecting a new round of

jokes about City and the game with Forza later in the week. Something to get under Danny's skin.

But he could take it. He could take anything Theo Gibbs threw at him.

'Great party,' Theo said again, still whispering.

Danny stepped to the side to push past Theo. But Theo moved across the doorway with him. Danny could sense more people behind him, waiting to get in. He could feel the tension rising. What was Theo up to? He clearly had something to tell Danny. But what Theo said next was not what Danny was expecting at all.

'I had a great time with Charlotte,' Theo said, stressing her name. 'She's a friend of yours, yeah?'

Danny said nothing. He just looked at Theo and saw a smile creeping across the sixth-former's face before he finally moved out of Danny's way.

Danny walked into the classroom. His head felt like it was about to explode.

What was Theo on about?

What the hell did that mean?

Was he going out with Charlotte now?

He kept his eyes on the pale green plastic tiles of the classroom floor. He followed the route through the tables that he followed every day. To his desk. And he looked at the desk. How the edge had been scuffed and chipped.

And then, as soon as the teacher came in, he closed his eyes and wished he'd just walked.

Back down the corridor.

Back across the grounds.

And out.

Out of school.

He'd do it in ten minutes, after registration.

He didn't even know if Charlotte was in the room. He didn't look.

SILVER CAR

Danny rushed across the school playing fields and out of the grounds towards the shops. He didn't look back. If someone was going to try to stop him, they wouldn't be able to anyway. He could do anything he wanted: his mum and dad were splitting up. No one could tell him what to do any more.

What now?

He couldn't go home. Dad was there. And he'd just send him back to school.

It was a shock when the silver car's door opened right in front of him.

'Get in,' a man's voice said.

For a moment Danny panicked. He was always on his guard. After he'd been involved with stopping crazed football chairmen, agents and billionaires getting what they wanted, there was always a chance a car would draw up to him somewhere and that something bad could happen.

So he sidestepped the car door and headed on.

'Danny?'

Danny stopped this time. He recognized the voice.

He turned. It was his friend, the football journalist, Anton Holt.

'Want a lift?' Holt said.

'OK. Where are we going?'

'Wherever you want. I tried to catch up with you before you got into school.'

'Town?' Danny said. He had decided to spend the day doing research for his project. 'I'm going to the library,' he explained. 'Researching something.'

'Will you have a coffee with me first?' Holt asked.

'On one condition,' Danny said.

'Anything.'

'We don't talk about all the stuff that's going on at home.'

Danny watched Holt frown, then take a breath.

'But I want to help you,' Holt said. 'To talk about it.'

'I don't need help.'

'Just talk,' Holt said.

'There's nothing to talk about. How's Emily?'

'She's OK,' Holt said, smiling.

'Well, that's everything sorted, then.'

'But she's worried about you.'

'Are you going to the thing tonight?' Danny said, changing the subject for a second time.

'Yeah,' Holt answered. 'You?'

'Yeah.'

Danny spent the day in the city library, going through books and newspapers for anything he could find out about Salvatore Fo. He'd discovered quite a lot.

That Fo wanted to become leader of Italy. That he modelled himself on Mussolini. That he wanted to drill for oil in the Mediterranean, and blow up mountains in the Alps to find precious stones. That he had a posh house in the Italian Lakes. That he might have killed political rivals. Or had them killed. But there was no evidence to convict him.

Danny needed more. More information. More time.

But he was gradually building something. He was getting happier about it.

Later, his dad met him at a café for something to eat before they went to the meeting about the City takeover.

Danny knew there was a reason for this – and Dad didn't waste time.

'Can we talk now?' Dad asked.

'OK,' Danny said.

'I want to know that you're all right. About home.'

'I'm OK,' Danny repeated. 'I feel weird and sad, but my heart's still beating.'

'This is going to be a hard time,' Dad went on. 'But I want you to know that your mum loves you and that . . .' Dad's voice broke. He was too emotional to speak.

'I know she loves me. I know you love me. But . . .' Danny stopped.

'But what?'

'But the problem is you don't love each other.'

'We do.'

'No, you don't,' Danny said.

'We do. It's just . . .'

'Then why don't you stay together?'

'We want different things,' Dad said.

Danny felt a sharp pain in his head. It came out before he could stop himself. '*She* wants different things,' he said, too loudly.

'No.' Dad was fierce now. 'Don't blame her. If you want to blame anyone, blame us both. Your mum has worked hard to keep this family together since my accident. She's worked too hard. She's carried us.'

'You've carried us too, Dad.'

'We all have,' Dad said. 'We're a family.'

'We *were* a family.'

Dad did not answer that.

It was getting dark when Danny and his dad met Anton at the Playhouse Theatre.

By the time the journalist arrived, there were dozens of men and women coming towards the theatre from all directions. Danny felt a gentle rain starting to fall.

'We'd best get inside,' Anton said. 'It'll be standing room only.'

As they went in, Anton filled Danny and his dad in on the gossip from the club in the lead-up to the Forza game. Holt was due to interview Sam Roberts the next morning – for Wednesday's pre-match edition of the paper.

Then Dad held Anton up.

'Get us some seats, Danny,' he said. 'I just want a word with Anton.'

Danny grinned at Anton. He knew what this was. This was Dad laying down the law about Emily. He knew his dad would be nice about it, but he also knew that Dad would be saying that if Anton didn't treat his daughter right, he'd be for it.

The theatre was packed. Danny got three seats at the back. He was pleased. He wanted to watch what was happening on stage, but he also liked to watch the audience. So sitting at the back was perfect.

Danny felt great. There was an atmosphere. It was the same feeling you got before kick-off at City FC.

Dozens of conversations.

Laughter.

Tension building.

'That's Phil Haxford,' Holt said, having led Dad through the packed seats. 'He's behind the whole protest movement. He used to run the supporters' club for City, but they sacked him after Gawthorpe disappeared.'

'Who are the others?' Danny asked.

Three other men were on the stage, all fiddling with microphones as the lights on the stage kept fading in and out.

'One's Don Kelner. He runs Radio City. He'll be chairing the meeting. Then there's David Brass – he writes on football and business for the *Guardian*. And that other guy . . . he looks like someone I've not seen for a long time.'

'Who is it?' Dad asked.

'Billy Giles,' Holt answered. 'He played for City in the sixties.'

Dad smiled. 'I wish I could see him. I watched

him play at the end of his career. What does he look like now?'

Danny studied the man on the stage as he eased himself into a black chair. He looked nothing like the photos Danny had seen of him in club history books, towering up for headers in the penalty area forty years ago.

'Small. Grey hair. Wearing glasses. But he looks fit,' Danny said.

Then they were called to order.

The meeting was fascinating to Danny. And he found a lot of things out.

First, that City had not had a legal owner since the death of Sir Richard Gawthorpe.

Second, that several organizations had tried to take the club over. City were in the Champions League. Lots of people wanted to own them.

Third, that no one could take the club over, because no one was really sure that Gawthorpe was dead.

But that was about to change.

A lawyer had found a way to prove that Gawthorpe was *legally* dead, meaning that City FC could now be bought.

The panel onstage were taking questions coming from every part of the theatre.

'It's all very well talking about this, round and

round,' shouted a man two rows in front of Danny. 'We've talked. We've invaded the pitch. We've done everything. But City are about to be bought out by these idiots.'

'We just have to keep at it,' Phil Haxford said. 'More of the same.'

'No!' shouted the man who had asked the question, followed by a burst of applause. 'It's time for action.'

'But what sort of action?' Billy Giles, the ex-player, said suddenly.

'Violent action,' the man in the crowd said, followed by more applause and shouting. 'This is *our* club and if we have to fight to keep it, then we have to fight.'

Danny sensed a sudden darkening of the mood in the room. Something bad could happen now. He could feel it.

'Violence never works,' the *Guardian* journalist said.

Several people in the audience started to boo.

Don Kelner, as chair, was trying to take control, but he was drowned out by noise and disagreement in the audience and on the stage.

Then Billy Giles stood up.

He did not speak or shout, but, even so, the audience fell silent.

Danny smiled. It amazed him that a room full of fans and experts would fall silent because a man who used to play football forty years ago had stood up. But they had.

'This is the most important moment in the history of City FC,' Giles said. 'The decisions you make tonight will determine the future of your club – if it even *has* a future.'

There was a murmur of agreement in the audience. Then silence again. In fact, it was so quiet, you could hear the cars on the roads outside.

'What you need is a figurehead,' Giles said. 'Someone associated with City FC, who can take the club on directly in the media and in person. Someone who will make a big news story every day because everyone will want to hear what they have to say.'

'How about you, Billy?' the chairman asked in a low voice.

'Not me. I'm not a big enough name,' Giles answered. 'It needs to be one of the players of today.'

'But none of them will do it,' the *Guardian* journalist said. 'They'll be watching their backs. If they stand up to the club, they'll get sacked. And they might not get another club if people think they're troublemakers.'

The room went quiet again.

There were no solutions.

Everyone had run out of steam.

Danny led his dad and Holt out of the theatre. The mood was just like it was after City had lost a key match at home. A cup quarter-final, something like that.

Danny was turning over all the things he'd heard in the theatre in his mind. There had to be a way out of this. But what? He ran a couple of ideas – bad ideas – through his head. Then he stopped walking, forcing Holt and Dad to run into him.

'What's up?' Holt asked.

'You know you said you were interviewing Sam Roberts tomorrow?' Danny asked.

'Yeah,' Holt answered, cautious.

'Can I come?' Danny asked.

'I suppose so. Once the interview's over,' Holt replied. 'Why?'

'There's something I need to ask him.'

'What?'

'If he'll do it.'

'Do what?'

'Be the person,' Danny smiled. 'The person Billy Giles was talking about.'

And he could see that his dad was nodding. 'And you're the perfect person to ask him,' Dad said. 'You saved him when Sir Richard Gawthorpe kidnapped him. He always said he owed you a favour.'

Danny nodded too. That was what he was hoping for.

TUESDAY

SAM ROBERTS

Danny arrived early at the bar where Holt had said he was meeting Roberts. He could see Holt and Roberts inside, talking.

Holt had told him to come in at 11 a.m.

The bar was attached to one of the area's poshest hotels, the Devonshire, which was owned by a very rich family.

Danny sat on a bench outside. He smiled. He'd been here before.

This was the place where, several months ago, he and Holt had met Alex Finn, the City keeper. That day someone tried to murder Finn, which started off one of the craziest cases Danny had worked on: a Russian billionaire bent on killing England keepers, helped by Sir Richard Gawthorpe.

He was thrilled to be meeting Sam Roberts again. The first time he'd met the famous footballer was just after he'd rescued him from the kidnap ordeal, and he'd come to thank Danny. When he was still a City player. Now, of course, he was Forza FC's star player.

Danny was distracted from his memories by a knocking sound. He looked round. Holt was banging on the window from inside the bar. And outside, Sam Roberts was walking towards Danny, his hand outstretched.

Danny couldn't quite believe it. One of the most gifted and famous footballers in the world had taken the trouble to come out to meet him. Not just wait for everyone to come to him.

'Danny?' Roberts said. 'It's great to see you again. How are you?'

'Great, thanks.'

'And your family? Your dad?'

'Fine too, thanks,' Danny said, although he did wonder why he'd said that. They were *not* fine. But he could hardly tell Sam Roberts about his mum and dad. You were just meant to say you were fine when people asked you how you were.

'Anton says you want to ask me something,' Roberts said.

'I do,' Danny replied.

'Whatever it is, I'll do it.'

'I won't hold you to that,' Danny laughed.

'Try me,' Roberts insisted. 'I owe you a lot.'

Danny shrugged.

'I do,' Roberts went on. 'You saved me from being kidnapped. You worked it out. You came in to find me. You took on Sir Richard and his armed guards. You were captured and they were going to kill you. And, after all that, you got none of the glory for it. I've never forgotten that. And I never will.'

As they walked across the gravel towards the door, Danny told Roberts about the meeting the night before. And about what Billy Giles had suggested.

Roberts nodded.

'And I think you would be a great person to do it,' Danny said.

They had just come to the door of the bar, when Danny had finished. Immediately Roberts stopped. And Danny wondered if he was offended.

'I'm sorry,' Danny said. 'I shouldn't have asked you. It's not fair.'

'No,' Roberts said. 'It *is* fair.' But then he fell silent.

They stood outside the bar for over a minute saying nothing. Danny knew to keep quiet. Roberts was thinking. He should leave him to it.

A bus drew up on the gravel of the car park.

Danny watched Roberts look over at it.

'I need to be on that bus,' Roberts said in a quiet voice. 'Light training before the game.'

'It's going to be odd for you playing at City,' Danny said.

'I know,' Roberts answered. 'I'll be honest with you, I'm nervous.'

'What about?'

'The fans. How are they going to react to me – after I transferred to Forza?'

'Don't worry about that,' Danny said.

'Really?'

'They still really admire you. You'll get the best welcome any City player's ever had coming back.'

Roberts nodded. 'I hope so. I miss City.'

Then Danny started thinking about Forza and Fo.

'You know Forza?' Danny asked.

'Yeah?'

'Are you happy there?'

'Oh yeah,' Roberts said. 'It's a great club.'

'Don't you think it's a bit strange there?' Danny asked. He wondered if Roberts had anything to say about it.

Roberts smiled. 'I suppose it is. It feels like Forza are going to be the biggest club ever. Everywhere we go everyone supports us. That's weird.'

'What's Fo like?' Danny asked. 'I'm doing a school project on him.'

'I've barely talked to him, to be honest,' Roberts admitted.

Danny felt disappointed.

'But I can say one thing,' Roberts went on. 'He's obsessed with TV. And adverts on TV. He knows everything about them. That's definitely weird.'

Danny nodded. 'Thanks. And I'm . . . I'm sorry I asked you to do that thing. It was too much to ask.'

Then Roberts was shaking his head. 'No, it's not too much to ask. And I wouldn't do it for anyone else. But, Danny, *you* saved my life. I always said, if I could do anything for you, I would. And I will.'

'You *will*?' Danny grinned. He felt elated.

'I will. But,' Roberts paused. 'Can it wait until after the two City–Forza games?'

'Yes. Of course.'

Danny didn't have time to thank Roberts any more. Holt was next to them and Roberts was picking up his training bag.

'Sorted?' Holt asked.

Danny nodded. And the three of them shook hands.

Roberts turned just before he left for the coach.

'Danny? Can you and your dad make it to Forza for the match next week?'

'I doubt it,' Danny said.

'I'll cover it,' Roberts offered, now crossing the car park to the coach. 'Flights, hotels, tickets. You'll be my guest. You can come to the players' lounge after the game. My treat.'

'Say yes, you idiot,' Holt said.

And Danny nodded. 'Yes,' he said. 'Yes please.'

WEDNESDAY

CITY VS FORZA

Town was packed with football fans, everyone wearing a scarf or replica shirt. Hordes of people were clustered outside pubs and cafés. Men with trolleys were flogging flags and banners. Touts were weaving among the crowds, asking for tickets.

This was a Champions League semi-final. Matches didn't come much bigger than this. Danny felt amazing. But something in the atmosphere seemed different today.

Dad picked up on it straight away.

'What's going on?' he asked.

'Forza fans,' Danny said.

'Right.' Dad nodded. 'Real ones?'

'I don't hear them talking Italian,' Danny remarked.

'Nor me,' Dad said. 'Is that lad from your school around?'

Danny had told his dad about Theo. The football stuff; not the Charlotte stuff.

'No, he'll be sat at home watching it on TV,' Danny replied. 'He wouldn't know a football stadium from a car park.'

He watched Dad laugh. It was good to see. He knew his dad was probably as miserable as he'd ever been in his life. Maybe even more miserable than when he'd had the accident and lost his sight. Danny hadn't asked him. He was bursting to tell him about the invitation from Sam Roberts. But he wanted to choose the right moment, make his dad feel as happy as he could be.

They headed for the stadium. Danny couldn't bear the tension any longer. Once he started to feel like this about a game, he had to get inside the stadium, chant, shout, or at least just be there.

Football time.

The first half of the game was cagey. Both teams were too cautious to attack. And however much the City supporters sang, the game remained tight and tense. Danny was pleased that all the fans in the stadium gave Sam Roberts a good welcome. He'd have hated it if he had been wrong and they'd booed their former player.

Danny looked over to the directors' box, where

the officials from both clubs sat to watch the game. He wanted to get an image of Fo on his mobile phone for his school project. One that nobody else had. Preferably one where the Forza boss was looking evil. But there was no sign of the Italian.

Danny had not missed the fact that several Forza fans were sat in the City end. All wearing Forza scarves, all sitting there as if it was *normal* for them to be among the City fans. In fact, he was pretty sure that the man in front of him was a Forza fan, even though he had a City accent. Danny thought of Theo Gibbs and willed City to score. He dreamed of going into school tomorrow and not having to even speak to Theo. A glance would do it.

In the second half the game opened up. And Danny knew it was to do with the fact that it was raining hard now. Defending was tricky when the pitch was wet. The players didn't have as much time to stroke the ball around. They became worried about making mistakes.

So for the first twenty minutes after the break it was end to end.

City attacking, then Forza attacking.

Sam Roberts looked dangerous for Forza, but somehow the City defence kept him out.

And then it happened.

Just as the rain was easing off, City got a corner.

The ball was swung into the area and – rising above everyone – City's leading scorer, Anthony Owusu, headed it in. When the ball hit the back of the goal, a shower of water burst from the soaked net.

Danny grabbed his dad by his arm and shook him.

The noise from the crowd was so loud his ears were ringing.

1–0 to City in the semi-final of the Champions League.

Once the furore had died down, Danny gazed around him at the so-called Forza fans. Some of them looked annoyed, or were trying to ignore the jibes of the City fans sat near them. Others were still smiling, as if they didn't know or care what it meant if their team won or lost.

Danny shook his head: he would never understand these people.

Now – as so often happened when a deadlock is broken – the game became very different. Danny felt he could sense the City players' increased confidence; a one–nil lead in the first leg of a Champions League semi-final was a brilliant result.

If City could hold on, Forza would have to beat them by two clear goals in Italy, because of the away goals rule.

The tension on the pitch had infected the fans

too. Now there was less singing. Everyone was on the edge of their seats. Literally.

'Come on, City!'

'Attack. Don't defend!'

'Keep them out.'

There was no noise from the other team's fans. Neither from the English Forza fans nor those from Italy.

With five minutes to go, the City manager made a substitution. Anthony Owusu was coming off, Kofi Danquah coming on.

Danny grinned. He knew Kofi. They were friends. They had met when Kofi had come to England from Ghana.

'Come on, Kofi!' Danny shouted, his words swallowed into the chaos and noise. 'Get us a second goal.'

And just before the end of normal time, Kofi got his chance.

Another corner.

Another melee in the penalty area.

The ball fell to Kofi.

If he could score this, Danny thought, the tie would be as good as over and City would be close to the Champions League final.

Plus Theo Gibbs would have to keep his mouth shut for a year at least.

Kofi hit it perfectly.

The ball rose towards the top corner of the Italian net.

Danny was convinced it was going in.

But the Italian keeper had other ideas. He leapt across the goal and finger-tipped the ball on to the cross bar.

Danny watched the next thirty seconds unfold in horror.

After hitting the cross bar, the ball ricocheted in the direction of the halfway line, such was the velocity of Kofi's strike.

The City defence was caught out.

Badly.

Too many City players were out of position: too many Forza players were ready to attack.

Danny watched as four Forza players attacked the City goal, Sam Roberts among them. Only three City defenders had made it back.

If Forza scored this, they'd be massive favourites to win the tie.

City could not afford to let this one in.

The Forza players were passing the ball at pace, but the game seemed to move in slow motion for Danny now as the City players struggled to keep up. Sam Roberts was bearing down on goal.

But *one* City player did manage to keep up: Kofi Danquah.

Now it was Sam Roberts against City's keeper and Kofi.

Danny watched, holding his breath, as Roberts rounded the keeper and slid the ball past him towards the goal.

People in the crowd screamed as they watched Kofi chase the ball to try and stop it going in the net.

He reached it, deflecting it.

The next second seemed to Danny to take a minute at least.

Kofi's clearance missed the empty goal, but hit the post.

Then the ball came back to Kofi. Bounced off his knee. And into the net.

An own goal.

City FC 1, Forza FC 1.

Disaster.

The man in front of Danny was now standing up. Danny had been right. He *was* a Forza fan. A so-called fan. He had his arms outstretched and was turning to catch the eye of everyone in the seats around him.

But he was not alone. There were hundreds of them. All around the stadium. All celebrating Forza's goal.

'Has it been disallowed?' Dad asked, sensing that around him people were standing up.

'They're Forza fans,' Danny explained, in a low voice. 'Everywhere.'

Danny noticed that several fights were breaking out now. And that the stewards were sprinting in to intervene.

Then he looked over at the giant screen in the corner. First, at the image of Kofi being helped to his feet by Sam Roberts. Rather than celebrating the equalizer, Roberts had his arm round the seventeen-year-old Ghanaian's shoulders and was consoling him.

Danny thought about the return leg and how he had been hoping City would win 1–0 and that he could break the news to his dad that they had tickets.

But the moment had gone.

Then the giant screen changed to a different image.

A man emerging from the directors' box. A man Danny knew well.

Salvatore Fo.

The Italian was nodding. Nodding like he knew Forza would score that goal.

Nodding like it was right that Forza were favourites to beat City now.

And Danny was filled with a rage that he struggled to keep control of. But he did.

For now.

When Danny and Dad got home after the City–Forza match, they told Mum about Sam Roberts and his offer. An all-expenses-paid trip to watch the second leg.

Mum smiled and said she was really pleased for them. Like Danny had expected her to.

He and his dad were going on an adventure.

Then Dad did something weird.

'Why don't *you* go, love?' he asked his wife.

'Me?' Mum reacted, sounding shocked.

'So long as Danny's happy,' Dad went on. 'I mean, you're learning Italian. And *I* got to go to South Africa with Danny. This would be perfect for you. It makes sense.'

Danny watched his mum and dad's exchange with interest. This was the first time they'd talked nicely together – without that underlying tension – for weeks. Maybe months.

His dad was being kind and his mum was pleased.

'Danny?' Dad asked. 'Is that OK?'

'Yes,' Danny said, nodding to his mum. Maybe it *was* OK. His mum *was* learning Italian. It would be good for her. And it meant Dad had been able to do something nice for her too. And maybe that was even more important.

These were the kinds of things that stopped parents splitting up.

Later that night, Danny stayed up to watch the highlights of the game on TV. He wanted to watch Kofi's own goal in detail. He froze the frame a few times, to see it unfold.

One time he did this, a strange thing happened. A message came up on the TV. Just green words on a black background:

SUPPORT FORZA FC.
YOUR TEAM.
YOUR SUCCESS.

Without thinking, Danny hit the play button. He lost the image immediately.

And, however much he tried to rewind and fast forward, he couldn't get it back.

PART TWO: ITALY

TUESDAY

ANOTHER COUNTRY

When Danny stepped on to the balcony of the hotel he was hit by the heat and light of Italy in early summer.

It was hard to believe that he was here, gazing across a beautiful lake at snow-capped mountains, in one of Europe's poshest hotels.

But it was true. He *was* here. And it was thanks to Sam Roberts.

'Danny?' a voice said from within the room. 'Have you seen the bathroom? It's amazing.'

Danny turned his eyes away from the view and went back into the cool shade of the hotel room, with its smart chairs, sweeping curtains and fancy lamps.

Danny's mum emerged from the bathroom grinning and Danny thought her face looked like a child's, full of excitement.

'The hand wash smells amazing,' she said. 'It's really expensive.'

Danny smiled. His mum looked well. They'd spent two hours sitting in a café in Milan before heading up to the lake and she had already caught the sun.

But there was something else about her. Instead of looking sad, like she had been at home recently, she looked relaxed and happy. Like she used to look when Danny was a little boy.

It had been a hard time for her, Danny realized that. He knew his mum and dad had been suffering. And seeing his mum all relaxed and suntanned like this made him appreciate a bit more about how unhappy she'd been.

'Look at the view,' Danny suggested, clearing his mind of the sadness that was starting to overcome his good mood.

His mum followed him on to the balcony. She gasped. 'Oh, this is beautiful. So beautiful. Thank you for bringing *me*. I feel so privileged to be here. Thank you, Danny.'

Normally, whenever Danny travelled to watch football – or solve football crimes – he went alone or with his dad. Coming with his *mum* felt weird. Mainly because it was the first time they'd been away together alone. But also because of something else. Something strange and uncomfortable that Danny couldn't even put into words.

Basically, Danny didn't like sharing a room with his mum.

Not in a hotel.

He knew they shared a bathroom at home. But this was different.

And he wasn't quite sure why.

'I could get used to this,' Mum said.

They were sitting on their hotel balcony together. A tray of drinks, sandwiches and cakes had been delivered by room service, accompanied by a welcome message from Sam Roberts.

'Are there any older players you think might take a shine to me like Sam Roberts has to you?' Mum went on.

Danny shrugged. He didn't know what to say to that. He didn't like to hear his mum say things about other men. Even if she *was* joking. He didn't like her talking about girls with him either. If she ever asked about his friendship with Charlotte, he always felt embarrassed and tried to change the subject.

There was an uneasy silence between them until Mum broke it by asking, 'Do you want to talk about me and your dad?'

'Not really,' Danny replied, trying to smile at her.

'Are you sure?' Mum went on.

'Maybe later?' Danny said.

'OK,' Mum conceded, her voice changing, sounding brighter. 'Then shall we plan what to do for the rest of today?'

Danny sat up in his chair and nodded. He was happy not to have to talk about his parents. He was worried things he could say might make matters worse. He'd already caused his mum and dad a lot of problems.

'What do *you* want to do?' Danny asked. They had all afternoon and evening, and most of the next day too. The match was not until the following evening.

Mum gazed out across the water. 'I want to go *there*,' she said.

The lake was bigger than any Danny had seen before. Their hotel was situated at the centre of the east shore and the lake stretched for almost twenty miles both north and south. There were probably seas that were smaller. The hills on the other side of the water were covered in deep, lush forest with villages dotted along the waterline and higher up. And behind *them* were snow-capped mountains: the Alps.

The sun was shining off the lake, creating a million ripples of light. Danny watched steamers and yachts skimming across the water like insects.

Danny's mum was pointing across all of this to the other side of the bay. At an outcrop of rock covered in trees, with three or four buildings spread out along the edge of the water. These were not just any buildings. They looked like palaces, their stone the colour of honey baking in the sun. Mum indicated the one on the far right.

'To that house?' Danny asked.

'It's a villa,' Mum said.

Aston Villa came into Danny's head, but he didn't bring it up. He knew his mum was as interested in football as he was in bathroom hand wash.

'A very rich person's house,' she continued. 'But normally the owner only comes in the summer, so tourists can have a look round the rest of the time. And I've been watching . . .' Danny's mum's voice was sounding excited now. 'The boat bus has been going from here to there. Tourists getting on and off.'

'Let's go then.' Danny got to his feet.

'Just let me sort myself out in the bathroom,' Mum said.

So Danny sat back down.

THE VILLA

The small ferry arrived at the hotel jetty almost immediately, meaning Danny and his mum did not have to stand in the stifling heat for too long.

Once a wooden gangway had been slipped into place, a man in uniform took Mum's hand to help her aboard, smiling at her like he fancied her. Danny was already getting tired of Italian men flirting with his mum. He'd heard this would happen and it had. At the airport. At the station. In the hotel. He had only ever seen his mum as his mum, not as an attractive woman. And it was weird that, because his dad was not there, this was happening.

Soon they were off, the small boat skimming the surface of the lake. Danny gazed at the enormous houses and gardens that bordered it.

The boat stopped first at a small village, then headed towards the villa Mum wanted to visit.

A large house with two small outbuildings

hidden by trees, it was completely isolated from all the other houses around. Danny looked at it as they approached, trying to work out how you would reach it by road. The hill was so steep behind it – a sheer rock face – that he thought that cars probably couldn't. Maybe it was only accessible by water?

It was an amazing place. More amazing than the other buildings Danny had been looking at.

And he started to feel quite glad they'd come.

There was something about this place. Something that excited him.

One hour later, he was bored out of his mind.

The house looked pretty good, as old houses went. The gardens were nice with their sculptures and tall thin trees. The views of the mountains were spectacular. But *inside* it was just like a museum. A load of paintings and statues. And Danny had never really liked museums.

Mum, however, was enjoying herself. She was talking to one of the guides about the paintings. In Italian.

And, to make things worse, every minute or so she would stop and tell Danny what she had found out. Danny could feel his legs getting heavier and heavier as they walked round.

One picture had been painted by someone who had been taught to paint by Michelangelo, she told him. And another had been on display in a famous New York art gallery.

Danny nodded and smiled.

After one long Italian conversation in a room full of paintings made up of small blotches of colour that Danny thought were rubbish, Mum attempted to explain them to him.

'They're by a Brazilian artist called Tomassina Tremezzo,' Mum said. 'Can you see what they're about?'

'Nothing?' Danny suggested.

Mum smiled. 'Look again,' she said.

Much as he loved his mum, Danny did not want an art history lesson. Especially not about *these* pictures.

'They're blotches,' Danny confirmed. 'I could do them with a pack of kids' paints from Tesco in an afternoon.'

Mum smiled. 'Can't you see? Half close your eyes, so it goes blurred.'

Danny squinted at one of the pictures. 'Still nothing.'

'See?'

'No.'

'You're just not trying,' Mum said.

'Blotches,' Danny replied.

'If you look carefully, Danny,' Mum was using her teacher-like voice now, 'you can see it's a picture of Jesus.'

'Jesus?' Danny said. Too loudly.

Several people in the quiet gallery looked round.

Mum nodded enthusiastically, not noticing. 'It's called subliminal art. The owner has bought dozens of these. Apparently he is a big fan of Tremezzo. Do you want to know what subliminal art is, Danny?'

'Not really,' Danny answered.

'Well, it's your loss,' Mum replied.

'Is there a café?' Danny asked. 'Or a gift shop?'

In the gift shop, as his mum was looking through some posters by the artist she liked, Danny watched a six-year-old girl with blonde ringlets who was looking at a book. She was leafing through it gently, being really careful with it. But then the woman behind the till rushed up to her and snatched it off her, saying, 'No, no, no!' and shaking her head.

The little girl looked upset. And Danny felt like telling her she'd done nothing wrong, that the woman in the shop was mean. She probably thought children shouldn't be allowed books. It made Danny want to leave even more quickly.

Then Mum was next to him, a framed picture in her hands. A copy of one by the blotch artist.

'What do you think?' she said.

Danny looked at the picture and its blotches.

'Mmmmm,' he said. 'How much is it?'

'You sound just like your dad,' Mum said. 'But I don't care. I like it, so I'm buying it.'

'Good,' said Danny. 'Then can we go and get a drink and some cake?'

The café overlooked the lake, just like their hotel room. It was surrounded by trees bearing oranges, and huge vases spilling flowers on to the terraces.

There was a breeze coming off the lake that made the heat outside bearable.

Mum was wearing a huge grin, holding her framed picture in front of her at different angles.

'Apparently,' she said, 'this house is the only place you can get copies of these pictures. I am so glad you brought me here.'

'And so am I . . .' The voice came from the next table. A deep Italian voice.

Danny turned to look.

A man was sitting with the sun behind him, so it was hard to see him clearly. But Danny could tell that he was smartly dressed, was about sixty or seventy years old and had brown hair.

'Do you like the picture?' the man asked Mum, in a strong Italian accent, leaning towards them.

'I do. I really do,' Mum gushed.

'May I join you?' the man asked. 'I know a little about her pictures.'

Mum nodded, catching Danny's eye. 'Yes. I'd love to know more about her work. I'm Samantha, by the way.'

Danny frowned. Here was *another* Italian man flirting with his mum. Now he was going to have to watch it up close and for a while. He sighed and gazed across the water, noticing that, up the lake, clouds were descending, a haze filling the valley. And that the breeze felt suddenly cooler.

The man shook Mum's hand, then turned to Danny.

Danny took his hand to shake it and looked up at the man. The sun had gone behind a cloud so now he could see him clearly.

He had to stop himself from snatching his hand away. Because the man on the other side of the table was none other than Salvatore Fo.

FRIEND OR FO?

Danny said very little for the first few minutes of the conversation that followed.

He was so shocked to be sitting opposite the man who was the focus of his school project, the man he had seen at City FC less than a week ago. A man he had started to hate.

He longed to get his iPhone out to take a picture for his project. But he couldn't. His hands were shaking too much.

Fo and his mum were now talking in Italian. Danny could tell Fo thought his mum's grasp of the language was poor. But he had to hand it to the Italian. He was being really nice about how she spoke. And he was helping her, teaching her the correct pronunciation. Also he had not boasted about who he was.

Maybe he was OK.

After a few minutes, Fo's mobile phone rang. He

excused himself and went to stand by some stone banisters at the edge of the lake. He leaned on a statue of a naked woman, occasionally gesticulating with his hands as he talked. Then he walked towards one of the smaller buildings that were higher up the hill, that looked like it was made up of three arches.

Mum gazed at him, then looked back at Danny and smiled.

'Nice man,' she commented. 'Do you think he'll come back?'

'You know who he *is*?' Danny interrupted, seething with irritation.

'No. He's just a nice man.' Mum beamed again.

Danny glanced round to check who was nearby.

'Mum,' Danny whispered. 'He's Salvatore Fo. He owns Forza FC. He owns several TV channels. He is one of the richest men in the world.'

Mum sat back in her chair, her eyes on Danny. 'Nooooo,' she said.

'Yes.'

'Are you sure?' Mum asked. 'Trust you to know all about him. I hope you're not going to start telling me he's an arch-criminal who wants to take over the world?'

Danny was about to reply to his mum's remark when he noticed a shadow over the table.

Fo was back.

'I apologize to you,' the Italian said in English. 'I had to go over to my offices to consider something.' He pointed over to the three-arched building. 'Please, Samantha. I have no appointments now. May I show you round my art collection? I would like to tell you more about my pictures. And understand more about you.'

'*Your* pictures?' Mum asked.

'Yes.' Fo bowed his head. 'I should introduce myself. I am Salvatore Fo. I am the owner of this house and of the art collection here.'

The next half hour was excruciating for Danny.

First, he had to look at the ugly pictures – again – and hear even more about them. Most of what the Italian said about them made no sense to Danny at all.

'For me,' he said at one point, 'they epitomize the twenty-first century. They show one thing, but in fact, deep down, they are doing something else. What might seem to a child to be just blotches are, to a sophisticated eye, an image of Christ.'

Danny thought he saw Fo look at him as he made the last remark.

Then he had to put up with Fo making jokes that were not funny – but his mum laughing anyway. And then the Italian kept touching his mum's elbow as he led her around the gallery. Danny watched him angrily and thought about his dad and how he missed him. Who did this Italian think he was?

Danny was rapidly losing the will to stand up.

Then, suddenly, in the middle of the tour, Fo turned to Danny. 'So, Danny, do you like *calcio*?'

Danny was about to answer that he did, but Fo broke in.

'This is our word, in Italy, for football,' he explained.

'I know,' Danny said.

'Danny loves football,' Mum interrupted. 'We're here to see his team play, in fact.'

'Ah. You are a Forza fan.' Fo moved across to Danny as if he was about to hug him.

Danny stepped back. 'No. I'm a City FC fan. I'm English. Why would I support an Italian team?'

Fo stopped and smiled. 'Maybe you like Forza a little? They are the biggest team in the world. Everybody should like Forza!'

Danny shook his head.

Fo smiled the same insincere smile he had been using on Danny for the last hour. 'One day I *think* ... how do you say? ... I *hope* you will change your mind.'

Danny smiled the same smile back.

'Never,' he said.

The art tour went on for another ten minutes before Danny managed to get away. He told his mum he was going to look round the gardens. He wanted some fresh air, he said.

She said he could go back to the hotel if he liked: she would see him there.

She barely noticed him leave.

Outside it was cooler now.

Danny sat around the back of the house, on a grass bank where the paths did not reach, meaning there were no other tourists around. Just him, the lake and the mountains. Behind him there was the building with three arches, and through one arch Danny could see a large white fan whirring through an open door. It was the place Fo had gone earlier. His offices, Danny remembered he had said.

He stared back across the lake, towards Switzerland. It looked very different up there now. He could no longer see the snow-capped mountains. Nor any blue sky. A dark dense cloud was rolling down, almost reaching the lake. And, in the distance, Danny heard rumbling. At home he would have thought it was a lorry going over potholes in the road. But there was no road here and he wondered if the sound was thunder.

Danny needed moments like this. Moments to sit and be quiet. If he did not find the time to think he could lose so many of the ideas he'd been having. First coming over to Italy. Then meeting Fo. And his mum flirting with the Italian. It was all too much. Now was his chance to sort it all out in his head.

But first he took his iPhone out. He wanted to text his dad.

We're by the Lake. We've met Fo. He's an idiot.
I miss you. D x

Then he sat back to think. He watched the clouds at the water's edge on the far side of the lake. The way the water was changing, turning black, choppy now.

That was when the thought came into his mind.

Danny glanced at the open door behind him.

What if he could illustrate his school project about Fo with pictures from the very man's offices? Pictures no one else had. That would be amazing. It would be like a piece of photojournalism that their media studies teacher was always going on about.

Danny got to his feet and glanced around him. No one around.

No sounds coming from the offices. They appeared to be empty.

He could be in and out within a minute. So long as he was quick, nobody would see him.

This could be *amazing*.

THE IMAGE

Danny walked across the lawn looking as casual as he could. He was just a tourist, a boy walking in an Italian garden.

His heart was already beating faster than it was meant to. But not so fast that he was feeling bad. He knew it was beating like this because his body had injected a massive dose of adrenalin into his blood. He had learned to cope with this. In fact, he loved the feeling. It was called being alive. And it beat looking round art galleries.

Once he had made it past the three arches, Danny found himself next to the door of the offices.

He glanced in. They *were* empty.

There was no time to lose.

It was a risk, but not a big risk. If he got caught he could just say he was looking for his mum who was a friend of Salvatore Fo.

Danny smiled and went in.

For the first few seconds he waited for his eyes to adjust. The offices were dark and gloomy. The room he found himself in was small with a high ceiling, the fan he'd seen through the doorway whirring round. There were three desks. All posh and made out of polished wood. A huge vase of blue flowers dominated one end of the room. At the other end, the wall was taken up by a massive oil painting of a huge bald man in a uniform.

Mussolini. The big, bald Italian dictator.

Danny activated his iPhone camera as he walked into the centre of the room. This was all perfect for his report. The picture of Mussolini was a great start. He had read a lot about this man who had been an ally of Hitler.

He snapped it.

He also took a photograph of another picture on the wall. A large map of the world, with three or four countries coloured green. Danny knew what this was too. He had read a bit about the history of Italy. This was a picture of the Italian Empire.

He started to wonder: why did Salvatore Fo have these pictures on the wall? Did they mean anything? What would he say about them in his school assignment?

As he was thinking, he heard a burst of voices outside. Instinctively he ducked down behind the flowers to observe a group of Germans walking past the doors of the offices.

Just tourists.

Once they had gone, Danny walked to the far end of the room to a doorway. He glanced through it. A corridor. Two closed doors and a narrow stone staircase.

Did he dare?

Yes, he dared. He *always* dared. Even though he knew he shouldn't be here and that he was taking an enormous risk.

He opened the first door. Inside there were two more doors. Toilets.

No need to go in there.

The next door in the corridor was locked. There was nothing Danny could do about that. He was not going to break in. So he left that alone too.

All that remained was the staircase. White-painted stone steps going up, Danny presumed, into the upper part of the arches in the building.

He listened before going up the stairs.

Nothing.

There was no one around.

Probably.

But he still took each step carefully one by one, thanking his luck that the staircase was built from stone and not wood, so there were no telltale creaks.

The door to the room at the top of the stairs was open.

But the room was empty.

Danny could tell that this was Fo's personal office. There were several pictures of the Italian with very famous people. Danny recognized some of them. Nelson Mandela. Tony Blair. And one of Fo with Barack and Michelle Obama, the three of them looking slightly uneasy.

He also knew immediately that he had to be careful. And quick. There was only one way into this room. The stairs. And that meant there was only one way out too.

He did not want to get cut off.

The desk on the far side was massive and took up half the space in the room. It was, Danny reflected, so big that it must have been made of an entire tree.

Danny snapped photos as quickly as his iPhone would allow him to. He tried to get everything in. The pictures on the wall. Some of the papers on the desk: he could blow them up later to see if there was anything interesting there.

He was about to leave when he noticed that

one of the drawers in the desk was slightly open.

He knew it was wrong to snoop, but he couldn't help himself. He was a detective, after all.

He knelt next to the drawer. There were some papers in there. And some other documents.

He glanced through them quickly.

Some were about football. Some not.

One thick file was labelled '1973 European Cup Winners' Cup Final', written in Italian and English. A covering letter at the front of the file said, 'Mr Fo – these papers demonstrate clearly that the referee of the 1973 European Cup Winners' Cup Final was bribed to ensure AC Milan won and that the true winners that year should have been the English team, Leeds United.' Danny photographed it. He would show it to Anton Holt. See what he had to say about it.

Danny carried on leafing through a series of images.

He flicked through them quickly, conscious he should be leaving soon to reduce his chances of being caught. And, as he did, he heard what he thought was another burst of thunder. Muffled because he was inside.

In the drawer there were pictures of players, stadiums, things to do with Forza FC. Most of them very familiar to Danny.

Nothing interesting.

Danny stood up. He was going to leave now. He had gathered some interesting pictures to illustrate his school report.

But then something flashed through his mind.

One of the images in the drawer was very familiar. Too familiar.

He knelt again next to the drawer.

He heard a toilet flush. But it didn't register with Danny immediately. He was too intent on the drawer and the image.

He found what he was looking for quickly.

And he almost fell backwards.

It was the same image as the freeze-frame he had seen on TV during the City–Forza highlights last week. The one that had puzzled him, but that he had not been able to find a second time, however much he tried.

SUPPORT FORZA FC.
YOUR TEAM.
YOUR SUCCESS.

What was this? Why was the same image he had seen on TV in a drawer in the desk of the owner of Forza FC?

Danny took his iPhone out, his hands trembling.

He needed to get a picture of the image.

As he did so, he heard a door bang.

Then footsteps on the stairs.

TRAPPED

Listening to the footsteps get louder, Danny wondered if he should hide or just pretend he was lost. A boy who thought he was in another part of the museum, that was probably the best idea.

But instinct told him to hide.

He dived under the desk. And because it was such a big desk there was plenty of room to conceal himself.

Once hidden, he concentrated on calming his breathing down. The shock of hearing someone coming up the steps had made him breathless. His breathing was noisy.

Deep breath in. Deep breath out. Once. Twice. A third time.

Danny managed to quieten himself just before a pair of smart trousers and men's shiny brown shoes appeared in his view. He could only see whoever it was that had entered from the waist down.

But it wasn't the shoes or the trousers that threw Danny. It was the gun the man was holding. And the fact that it wasn't just any gun, certainly not a pistol you might expect a security guard in Italy to be carrying. It was a semi-automatic machine gun. The kind Danny had seen the police at Milan airport carrying. A serious weapon.

The next question that came into Danny's head was: why? Why would a museum, an old house, need guards with machine guns?

Maybe it was normal in Italy. He couldn't be sure. He didn't know enough about the country. But it didn't feel right. It seemed so out of place.

Danny listened as a double crack of thunder sounded in the mountains above the villa.

And then his mind started working on full power.

The gun.

The image in the desk. The same one he'd seen on the TV.

Support Forza FC. Your team. Your success.

The pictures in the gallery downstairs.

What he knew about subliminal art.

And what had Fo said? *One day I think ... how do you say? ... I hope you will change your mind.*

Danny knew that he had stumbled across

something big. Something dangerous. It was a gut feeling. And he always trusted his gut feelings.

He watched as the man with the gun came closer to the desk. He heard him pick up a phone and gabble something in Italian. Then he put the phone down and moved away.

Danny recognized only the last word. *Catenacio*. Danny understood *that* word. It meant chained – or locked. An Italian style of football was named after it. He'd read about it in a book. The defence was meant to be locked like a door.

Was the gunman about to lock the door?

Now Danny had to make another choice.

Stay here and possibly – probably – get locked in.

Or run now, taking the guard so much by surprise that he wouldn't have time to use his gun.

Danny got up on to his toes and hunched under the desk like a sprinter in the blocks.

Somehow he had got himself into a situation that could be seriously dangerous for him.

This wasn't right. He had to get away. Quickly. This was it.

The man with the gun was still standing in the middle of the room, his feet pointing away from the door. Danny realized that this could win him time. The second or second-and-a-half that the man needed to turn around was all Danny needed to get himself halfway down the stairs.

He didn't wait to think it through any more. This was his chance.

Danny exploded from under the desk.

When he reached the door to the steps he heard the Italian man react.

First a shout. Then a metallic click.

The gun.

As Danny pounded down the narrow staircase he half expected to be stopped by the feeling of hot metal hitting his back, followed by the sound of gunfire.

But the two sounds he could hear were pounding footsteps and shouting.

He put them out of his mind so that he could focus on getting away, sprinting through the main office room, knocking the whirring fan over, to the alarm of a young woman with long brown hair who had been gazing into a mirror. The woman screamed, making Danny pick up his pace.

And now he was outside. In the light. In the fresh air.

At least they can't shoot me here, he thought. *There'll be too many people around.*

He hammered across the lawn, heading towards

the statues and the stone banisters on the edge of the lake.

That was when he started to panic.

Danny had been chased several times before. Sometimes, like this, by armed men. Because he was fast he had always got away, running along a track, on a path by a river, up a road.

But he had just realized that there was no way in by road here.

And no way in meant there was no way out.

Except by boat.

But there was no boat.

Danny stopped at the foot of the hill, caught in the shadow of the statue he had seen Fo standing beside earlier. He looked behind him.

Two men were coming down the hill.

But they weren't running. They were walking. That was because they knew that Danny had no way out.

Just like the man approaching from his left and the man approaching from his right would know.

Danny was surrounded.

He looked up towards the café terrace to see if his mum was there. But she wasn't.

A sudden rain shower had begun to fall. It *was* a storm. Thunder was ripping down the lake now. Danny couldn't see any of the mountaintops.

Rain clouds obscured them all. He couldn't even see the other side of the lake.

As a result, all the other sightseers had made a dash for the house – and the café.

Danny was on his own with the four men coming towards him.

What now?

He turned to the water. He had to make a choice. Allow himself to be caught? Or go over the wall?

DROWNING

Danny climbed over the stone banister and looked down.

It was a twenty-metre drop. He'd never dived that far before. There were rocks scattered in the water below. And it was rough now that the weather had turned, big waves hitting the edge of the mountainside. He could barely distinguish the rocks from the waves.

But he had no choice.

No choice at all.

The four men had stopped. They looked hesitant. As if they were trying to work out if the boy they had caught trespassing meant to jump – or if they could catch him without much trouble.

Danny shifted his footing.

It was a stand-off.

Nobody moved.

Then Danny felt his iPhone buzz in his pocket.

It would probably be a text from his dad. A reply.

If he jumped into the lake now he would never get to read what his dad had texted. And his phone would be ruined.

And then another thought occurred to Danny. The image he had photographed in Fo's office. He would lose *that* if he jumped into the water. And he felt sure that it was important.

He put his hand into his pocket, gripping his iPhone.

Suddenly, as if they could anticipate Danny's next move, two of the men started to move towards him. And they were both grinning. Like they were enjoying themselves. They knew that, in the driving rain, there was no one else about, or watching what was going on.

Discreetly, without being observed, Danny pulled his phone out and placed it on a ledge on the outside of the banister, making sure it was in a dry place, where the rain would not reach.

Then he launched himself into the water.

Danny could not think for the next few seconds.

First, he felt himself falling through the air. Then hitting the water. He had meant to land like he'd seen the Olympic diver Tom Daley land once, his feet meeting the water as if he was standing upright.

But it didn't quite work out like that.

Suddenly he was underwater and it was dark. Danny instinctively took a breath and his mouth filled with water. He felt his lungs explode with pain.

For a few seconds he didn't know what was up and what was down – or if he was drowning.

He could only feel panic and the thrashing of his limbs.

But that wasn't working.

So, rather than struggle, he stopped moving. He figured he would float to the surface if he did that. So long as he kept his mouth shut and didn't breathe in again.

It was a risk. But it felt right.

Within seconds he was on the surface.

He breathed in now. The air was beautiful. But he still wasn't quite sure where he was.

The lake was black and choppy. Waves pushed themselves over his head. And he noticed small explosions on the surface of the water. At first he feared they were bullets coming from the guards, but he realized quickly that they were just huge raindrops.

Now he had to decide what to do next.

He looked up to where he thought the villa was – where the men would no doubt be looking down at him.

But the rain was so heavy now that he could only make out the vague shape of the balcony. He couldn't see the men. So he assumed that, if he could not see them, they would not be able to see him.

That was good.

Hoping he was right, Danny started to swim. First to the edge of the rocks that he had seen from above. He grabbed one, waiting to get his breath back.

He was safe. Sort of.

But now he had to work out his next move.

Go back into the villa – making out he'd been soaked by the rain, not the lake – to see his mum?

Swim back across the water to the hotel?

Stay here?

He wasn't sure. He was still confused by the fall and by being in the water. If he went back into the villa anything could happen. There was no guarantee he would be safe.

And his mum was expecting that he might go back to the hotel.

He would swim across to the hotel.

That was the best thing to do.

Danny looked across the water. It was a little clearer out towards the hotel.

He knew he could do the distance. He loved swimming. He'd swum a lot in Lake Ullswater when he was younger, with his sister.

But what about his iPhone?

Danny looked up towards the villa and the balcony. There was a sheer rock face between him and where he had concealed his iPhone. There was no way he could climb that now. Especially as the four men would probably still be looking out for him.

That was a problem. A serious problem.

And then Danny started to feel cold. Really cold. He could feel a chill running through him.

He decided he could not get the phone now. He would have to come back tonight. After dark. It was the only way.

So Danny Harte released himself from the rock he was clinging on to, submerging himself back into the water of the lake. And he started to swim.

DINNER WITH MUM

'So how did you get *back*?'

Mum was quizzing Danny about the afternoon. And what he'd been up to.

They were having dinner in the hotel. The sun had come out again so they had decided to sit on the restaurant's terrace.

The hotel was fifty metres up the side of the mountain, but still next to the lake. You could see across the water to the small town on the other side. And to Salvatore Fo's villa.

Danny glanced at the villa, trying to focus in on the spot where he'd stowed his iPhone.

'I swam,' Danny answered.

'What? You swam?'

Danny saw no point in lying about that. So long as his mum didn't know about his other adventures – particularly the guns – why not tell her some truth?

'I went down to the water and it looked nice,' Danny said.

'Danny, that was dangerous. I wish … You could …'

'I kept to the edge,' Danny went on. 'I was never more than ten metres from land. I thought it would be fun. And I only swam for a bit. A family in a rowing boat gave me a lift back to the hotel.' He hated lying to his mum, but at least the last part was true.

Mum shook her head. Danny could sense she wanted to tell him off, but was restraining herself. To keep the peace, Danny thought.

A waiter arrived at the table. Danny fiddled with the silver cutlery, his Coca-Cola glass and his napkin while Mum ordered – in Italian – for both of them. He watched his mum. He had to admit that Italy had had a good influence on her. The lines that had been bunching around her eyes had almost disappeared, like her face was relaxing.

Danny decided it was time to change the subject. He wanted to find out more about the paintings his mum had been so interested in – and that Fo had been so obsessed with. He was convinced there was something about them that could help him work out the answers to his questions about Salvatore Fo. So when Mum looked back from the waiter, he started asking questions.

'Did you enjoy meeting Salvatore Fo?' he asked.

'I did,' Mum said, cautious.

'Did you *really* like those pictures?'

'You know I did, Danny.'

The wine waiter arrived and asked Mum to try the wine. She tasted a little and nodded to him.

'I thought they were rubbish,' Danny said, bluntly.

'Yes. You made that clear to Salvatore,' she smiled thinly.

'How much does he spend on them?'

'A lot,' Mum answered, putting her wine glass down. 'I expect they cost tens of thousands of pounds. Why don't you look the artist up on your fancy iPhone and see?'

Danny's heart skipped a beat. He tried hard not to show his shock. 'Erm . . . I didn't bring it down with me,' he replied. Then he changed the subject again. 'I get the idea you're meant to see something hidden in the blotches. But what's the point?'

'Do you really want me to tell you?'

'Yes,' Danny said, leaning forward.

'Well. It's called *subliminal* art,' Mum said, suddenly animated. 'On the surface, it looks like one thing – the blotches. But hidden from your conscious mind there is another image below. One that your mind sees, but your eyes don't.'

'How's that?'

'Well, your eyes take in information all the time. So much information that your conscious mind can only use some of it. But other things, which your conscious mind can't take in, go in anyway, but without you knowing.'

'And that's Jesus?'

'Yes. But if you really look, you can see him.'

'I see,' Danny said, wondering what this all meant to him. Not a lot so far. But he knew he had to find out everything about everything. He'd been reading the new Young Sherlock Holmes stories by Andrew Lane and Sherlock is told that he needs to gather as many facts as possible to help him solve crimes. That's what Danny was doing now.

The first course arrived. Small portions of food set out to look nice. But not to satisfy an appetite, Danny thought.

'Do you think this food is subliminal?' Danny asked his mum.

She laughed. A nice laugh. He liked making her laugh.

'Maybe,' she said. 'But, seriously, subliminal techniques have not just been used in art. In the sixties, when TV started showing adverts, some companies used to flash images during popular shows. Like, for a split second, a picture of a drink would come up. Then thousands of people would go and spend money on those drinks.'

Danny looked up sharply.

'But it's not a technique used any more, it's banned now. And it's . . .'

His mum carried on chatting but Danny was no longer listening. All he could think of was the image he had seen in Fo's desk. And his iPhone sitting under that wall across the water.

He *had* to get it back.

Because he'd worked out the answer to the most unanswerable of questions. Why everyone was supporting Forza FC.

But – before he thought about what that meant – he had to find a boat.

NIGHT BOAT

Danny had already identified the boat he was going to use. It was hidden under an arch on the waterfront, only visible from the ferry he'd been on with his mum. He was pretty sure it belonged to the hotel. He'd also spotted the crowbar he was going to use to get to the boat, among the gardener's tools at the back of the hotel.

He left through the back exit of the hotel, a fire door. That way he could avoid whoever was manning the reception desk. He set the back door slightly ajar, so that he could get back in.

It was 3 a.m. And dark.

Overnight, all the clouds had been sucked back into the mountains. The sky was clear now, but moonless.

A lovely cool breeze had blown away the heat of the day.

Danny walked down a cobbled alleyway to

reach the lakefront. All he had with him was a white towel and a small sealable plastic bag. He was wearing just a T-shirt, a pair of shorts and some black flip-flops.

There were no cars, no people, no boats. Just mountains and water and a thousand closed shutters.

He was alone with the night.

Danny loved it like this.

Once he reached the front he walked along the hotel jetty, carrying the crowbar. At the end he found a gate. On the other side he could see the rowing boat. Tied with a rope with oars propped inside it, it was ready to use. The only problem was that the gate was locked.

He'd imagined this would be the case. That was why he'd brought the crowbar. But, thinking about it, he decided not to use it. If he did it would damage the gate and he didn't want to do that.

He knew what he had to do next. He couldn't open the gate without damaging it. He couldn't climb over it. He had to swim round it.

But he was ready for that.

Danny took off his shorts, T-shirt and flip-flops, placing them through the bars of the gate. Then he dipped himself into the cool water of the lake.

Three minutes later he was in the boat, dry and dressed. Suitably refreshed.

He untied the boat and pushed off.

It moved as if it was floating on air.

Once he was out on the water – and he could see that nobody from the hotel was running down the jetty to shout at him – Danny started to enjoy himself.

He used the time to run through what he had worked out.

Huge numbers of people were supporting Forza FC across the world.

Danny had seen an image hidden in a replay of a football match, suggesting everyone should support Forza FC.

The owner of Forza FC (and of several TV channels) was obsessed with art that showed one thing, but communicated something else. Subliminal art.

What did all these facts add up to? That Salvatore Fo was using subliminal TV images to make everyone support Forza FC.

Danny was sure of it.

And that was why he wanted to get his phone back. That was where his evidence was.

The lake was beautiful. It reflected the black of the sky and the pinpoint light of the stars. He was enjoying the sound of the water as his oars cut through it. It reminded him of the holidays he had been on when he was young. Rowing with his dad. Finding somewhere to cast their fishing lines.

Forty minutes later Danny was feeling less at ease.

He wasn't sure if it was in his mind, but now that he was within a hundred metres of Fo's villa the air and the lake seemed colder. Much colder.

Danny shrugged off the feeling and concentrated on rowing as quietly as he could, dropping the oars into the water slowly, then pulling back on them with a steady strength.

There were no lights on in the villa. But Danny still had to take care.

He aimed his boat for the rocks, near where he had dived into the water to make his escape. It was hard to find the right spot, because the weather was so different now. But he knew he needed to be beneath the banisters.

Edging the boat close to the rocks, he leaned over and grabbed them. Then he clambered out, tying the boat's rope to the stump of a tree.

Danny took a moment to breathe in and out. This had gone well so far. Mainly because he had kept himself calm. He needed to be sure he sustained that. How many crime books had he read where the detective had *not* been calm – had been eager or angry? And every time that happened, something went wrong.

Danny was determined that *nothing* would go wrong tonight.

Once he was as focused as he needed to be, he started to make his way up towards the villa.

But the rocks were wet and slippery. He went slowly, knowing that as long as he got a good foothold he would be OK. He had read about climbing. Keep three limbs fixed to the rock face and move only one at a time and he'd be fine.

It didn't take long.

If he lifted his head now, he would be able to see the bottom of the stone banisters. And find his iPhone.

He put both his hands on the bottom of the banisters and pulled himself up.

He looked to his left, then edged along to the place where he thought his iPhone was. The silence was so perfect that he swore he could hear his heart beating.

No sign of his phone. He'd have to check the other direction.

Danny began to move to his right, hands on the banisters, feet on the black rocks.

Methodical. He had to be methodical.

'No, Meester Johnson, I do not want my name attached to the deal.'

Danny recoiled instinctively and nearly fell back into the water. He had to dig his fingers into the rock to rescue himself.

Someone was there.

And not just *anywhere*. He could now see a pair of dark trousers two metres from his face. On the other side of the banisters.

Danny lowered his head. Slowly.

As he did he saw another figure. A young woman, maybe eighteen or nineteen years old. Blonde, and wearing a small white dress.

Danny closed his eyes. Again he had to concentrate on breathing in and out to calm himself.

To stop himself from throwing up with fear.

To think.

And to listen. Because he knew whose voice he was hearing. Salvatore Fo.

'We take over the club. We use the same network of companies. The ones based in the Cayman Islands. The ones I use with Forza. But it would be so helpful, Meester Johnson, if you could arrange for City FC not to play beyond their abilities this evening.'

Danny nearly fell back again. What was this?

It was lucky Fo had his back to Danny because,

although he had managed to keep his footing, he had dislodged a stone.

He heard it make a distant plop as it hit the lake below.

Danny focused on holding on. He tried to think.

Fo had clearly had enough of the phone call. He had stopped talking and was now moving towards his young friend.

It was time to get out of here, Danny decided, not a time to think. He could think later. What he needed to do now was retrieve his phone.

Danny, taking a risk now, edged to his right. Was it there? He reached up and down, left and right, as gently as he could, to avoid knocking it off the ledge. Mercifully, when he found it, it was still dry. He wrapped it tightly in the plastic bag he had brought, sealed the top and stuffed it into his shorts.

Now all he had to do was get into the boat and row back across the lake.

As he started to descend he took one more look at the scene above him.

He was filled with horror by what he saw.

Although he could see that Fo still had his back to him, he could also see that the young woman was pointing.

Directly at Danny.

SEA MONSTER

Danny had no choice. He had to get out of there. Quickly. So, using all the power in his legs, he hurled himself backwards.

It had been instinct to throw himself backwards and not climb timorously down the rocks.

Self-preservation.

He did a back flip and straightened his body, arms out.

He'd seen Tom Daley do this too.

He hit the water feet first. And soon he was, once again, in the deep dark confusion of the water.

But this time he had kept his mouth shut. And this time he knew which way was up. So it wasn't as bad as the last time.

As he came back to the surface, all he had to worry about was whether Salvatore Fo had a gun.

Danny breathed in and looked up. He could see

two figures watching him. Fo and the beautiful girl. Neither of them had a gun. Neither of them was on their mobile phone. They were just watching him.

Danny stared at them staring at him while treading water, working out what to do. After a few seconds, he climbed out on to the rocks and into his boat.

He decided not to look up again until he was safe.

Once in, Danny pushed the boat away with one of the oars and started to row. Fast, this time. No more silent rowing. He was an Olympic rower, using all the power he had.

The boat moved speedily through the water. Because he was facing backwards, towards the villa, he could see Fo and the young woman on the balcony. They had still not moved. They were just watching him.

But Danny knew that that could just be appearances. Maybe Fo had a helicopter gunship heading down the lake towards him and it was a matter of time before it came round the corner like a huge and deadly night wasp. Or maybe he had a submarine forcing its way up from the bottom of the lake to smash his tiny rowing boat to pieces.

Danny felt like he was a character in some terrifying thriller novel. Alex Rider. Young Bond.

So he rowed.

Hard and fast, his upper arms and shoulders exploding with pain.

But he was strong. And soon he was halfway back to the hotel – and still nothing had happened.

No gunship.

No submarine.

Danny felt like laughing.

Was he safe?

He slowed his pace. His arms could not take much more, anyway.

And now, because his body was not working flat out, he could, at last, think.

What had Fo been talking about?

Danny could remember what he had said word for word.

We take over the club. We use the same network of companies. The ones based in the Cayman Islands. The ones I use with Forza. But it would be so helpful, Meester Johnson, if you could arrange for City FC not to play beyond their abilities this evening.

Take over which club?

He had to be talking about City FC, didn't he?

Who was Mr Johnson?

Was there a Mr Johnson involved in the takeover of City?

Arrange for City FC to do *what*?

And why should Mr Johnson expect to have control over City FC?

Then the hardest question of all came into Danny's head: was Fo involved in the takeover of City FC? As well as being involved in brainwashing millions of fans into supporting Forza FC?

Everything was still quiet.

Just the faint sound of ripples of water hitting the side of Danny's boat.

And Danny realized he had stopped rowing.

He was sitting in a tiny boat on an enormous lake under the light of half the stars in the universe. And everything was becoming clearer.

The image in Fo's drawer.

The image on the TV screen at home.

The reason his sister and Theo Gibbs and everyone else had become Forza FC fans.

Subliminal advertising.

Brainwashing.

It was a massive multi-billion-pound scam. And the only person who knew what was going on was Danny. And he was sitting on a lake in the dark, alone.

He had to get back to the hotel.

As all these thoughts ran through his head, Danny heard the first sound that was not the lapping of water or a creak of his boat.

It was the sound of an engine.

And, second by second, it was getting louder.

When first light hit the lake just before six that morning, an English family heading off on a fishing trip in a rowing boat spotted something in the water.

'It's a sea monster!' the youngest of the children shouted, delighted.

The mother steered the boat towards the shape. She was anxious, but not afraid. She knew it couldn't be a monster. She had already seen it was the underside of a small rowing boat.

When they arrived they found the boat and saw two oars floating nearby.

Also, a white towel, sodden, floating in the water like a ghost.

WEDNESDAY

FORZA FC

Danny was a bit disappointed when he came round the corner, through a dusty car park, to find himself face to face with the world-famous Forza football stadium. It was famous for being the newest, fanciest stadium that had been completed in less than a year only eighteen months earlier.

It had already been a long day for Danny. It had started with him capsizing his rowing boat at four in the morning, to make sure he would escape whoever was approaching him in the motorboat. Then, getting far enough away from the rowing boat before the motorboat reached it. He had achieved both and swam back to the hotel. Then, over breakfast, he had convinced his mum she didn't need to come to the match if she didn't want to.

The main thing had been to check his phone. Was it OK? Were all the images he needed on it? To his relief, the answer was yes.

There was no denying the stadium was big. And Danny recognized the famous crown design around the edge. But that was all. It did not have that magic feel of other stadiums he had visited like the Luzhniki in Moscow, Wembley in London or Elland Road in Leeds.

It was just a big concrete stadium.

But Danny *was* excited to be among thousands of City fans. He had travelled up with them on the Milan underground from the city centre, English football chants filling the corridors and stairways. Then they'd walked along a long road, next to a wall covered in graffiti, CAMPIONI D'EUROPA and CURVA SUD FORZA sprayed in blue aerosol paint.

The main song they had been singing was 'City Till I Die'. But other fans had been chanting 'Enger-land'.

As Danny walked, he texted Charlotte. One, because he missed her and wanted to check she was OK. Two, because he wanted her to find some things out for him.

Charlotte. Please will you do a survey for me at school? Ask people three questions. One, do they like football? Two, do they have satellite TV? Three, do they support Forza? I need 100 people at least. Love D xxx

Danny knew she would do it. She was amazing. She would probably ask 200 people and collate the results for him. All in no time using Facebook and various chat rooms. And she'd do it without wanting to know why.

This was how they were now. Danny and Charlotte. They could operate without having to ask loads of questions of each other. They'd been through a lot together.

Danny felt safe about this. But one thing he did not feel safe about was how Theo Gibbs was going to affect their friendship. But there was no time for thinking about that. Not now.

Danny left the City fans, who were being led to the right, and walked around the other side of the stadium to the main gates, like Sam Roberts had told him to. At the gate he showed a special pass that Roberts had left at his hotel and he was led in to be greeted by a young woman with dark hair and eyes. She reminded him of Charlotte.

'Theese way, Meester Harte,' the young woman said, leading him to a red-carpeted entrance. But that was about all she did say. And Danny wished he could speak Italian, so he would be able to say more than 'thank you' and 'please'.

There were thousands of people milling around, all wearing the Forza FC scarves and tops Danny had come to hate. But here they seemed OK. He didn't object to people supporting Forza in the city where they played. That was like him following City. What he *hated* was the fact that people like Theo Gibbs and six-year-olds in Brazil were becoming Forza fans.

Danny's mind quickly returned to Salvatore Fo. He was aware that he was entering a stadium where the big boss *was* his enemy and that it was a risk that he might see him again. But, as he had texted Anton Holt and arranged to meet him, that would be his safety net.

And he had a lot to tell Anton.

Anton met Danny in the players' lounge as soon as he heard Danny had arrived. Kick-off was less than half an hour away.

The lounge was a large room with a high ceiling. In England, Danny had been in three or four players' lounges – the place footballers came to after the game to relax and to meet the club's sponsors. They had been nice, but they always had low ceilings with polystyrene tiles like at school. Just plain rooms with pictures screwed to the wall, named after a famous player of the past that changed every few seasons. But *this* was nice. There were several marble tables around the edge of the room, laid out with drinks and food. Waiters, impeccably dressed, walked round with trays to serve the guests. There were dozens of posh sofas. Chandeliers. It was a bit like the hotel back by the lake.

'It's good to see you, Danny,' Anton said, holding a glass of water at his side. 'I can't really stop, but I'll catch up with you properly after the match. I have to sort out my notes for my match report now.'

'But there's something I need to tell you,' Danny said. 'I've found some stuff out.'

He felt slightly irritated by Anton. He'd already texted him to say that he had found out something big.

Anton looked Danny in the eye. He sighed. 'OK. I'm sorry. Tell me.'

This was Anton acknowledging that, in the past, he had ignored Danny's instinct for crime, maybe even treated him like a child.

'I went to Salvatore Fo's house,' Danny said quietly.

'You did what?' Holt nearly choked on his drink. 'Danny! Are you mad?'

Danny lowered his voice more. 'It's OK. I was with my mum. It was on a tourist trip.'

Holt led Danny to the corner of the room. Danny glanced over his shoulder out of a huge window. There he could see the pitch that he had seen on the TV. Under the lights, packed with tens of thousands of fans, the scene was breathtaking.

But Danny had some talking to do. He was not here to admire the view.

'Can we make this quick?' Holt said. 'Just give me the bones of it now. We can talk more after. OK?'

Danny nodded. This meant he had two minutes to tell Holt about what could be one of the greatest sporting crimes in the history of the world.

'Right,' he started. 'You know how everyone is supporting Forza in England?'

'I know how you go on about it,' Holt grinned.

Danny ignored the jibe, saying nothing.

'Yes, I do,' Holt conceded. 'I've been planning to write something about it.'

'Well, I think I know why it's happening.'

'Go on.'

'When I recorded the City–Forza game at home, I paused it to watch Kofi's own goal.'

'Right.'

'And it froze on a weird screen that said, "Support Forza FC. Your team. Your success."'

'Did it?'

'Yes,' Danny said, getting his iPhone out and showing Holt the image.

'That does look weirdly familiar,' Holt muttered, squinting.

'And when I sneaked into Fo's office . . .' Danny went on.

'What?' Holt put his hand to his head and his glass down.

'When I sneaked into Fo's office . . . I found the image in some papers.'

Holt nodded. He was listening now.

'And when my mum and I met Fo . . .'

'You met *Fo*? How? He's impossible to meet.' Holt looked astonished.

'When we met him, he – well, how can I put it – he fancied my mum and he showed her round his art collection. Like a load of blotches of nothing, that, when you squint at them and put your head on its side, you can see Jesus. He talked a lot about it. And I asked my mum about it. And she said it was called –'

'Subliminal,' Holt interrupted.

Danny nodded. Holt was staring out of the window. Danny knew this meant Holt was thinking. He also knew not to interrupt.

The players' lounge was quiet now. Most people had gone out into the executive boxes. Where Danny was meant to be sitting too. He gazed over at the City end. That was where he really wanted to be. With the real fans. So he could sing and chant and shout City on.

Holt glanced around nervously.

'Is there anything else?' he asked, in a low voice. 'The match is about to kick off.'

'Erm . . . I got chased by gunmen when they found me in Fo's office. I had to leave my phone there. So I went back in a boat at 3 a.m. and Fo was there and he was talking about something to do with City and the Cayman Islands and how he might be interested in buying the club out. Then he saw me. And I think I got chased. And I capsized my boat to escape.'

Anton Holt now had his head in both hands.

'I think,' he said, 'you'd better come and watch the match with me.'

FIRST HALF

Danny had watched a football match sitting in a press area before. In Russia. That day he'd had *two* crazed football chairmen to deal with. Today there was only one. And Fo was, thankfully, nowhere to be seen.

Danny sat next to Holt on a cushioned blue seat, a computer screen filled with facts in front of him. Holt explained to him it was provided by UEFA: up-to-the-minute match stats that journalists were free to use in their reports.

Both teams started cautiously, as they had in England.

It was 1–1 after the first leg. Forza would win on the away goals rule if the match ended 0–0, so the Italian team had no need to take risks. That meant City needed to score.

So Danny was increasingly delighted, as the

match went on, to see his team attacking more and more.

He was also happy to see his friend Kofi Danquah on the pitch. He had been worried Kofi would be dropped after his own goal in the first leg.

Danny was not happy, however, to hear from a section of the Italian fans when Kofi was on the ball. It was a kind of hooting noise. Danny knew it was racist chanting, that they were making the monkey noises you sometimes heard fans in Italy, Spain and Eastern Europe make. He was glad to see Kofi was not affected by them; in fact, Kofi was playing really well. Danny could see from the match stats on Anton's screen that Kofi had had the most touches of the ball and that he had completed the most passes.

After about fifteen minutes of football, Holt passed Danny a note. *Show me the image on your phone again.*

Danny showed him it.

Holt nodded and turned away.

Just as he did, Danny saw Kofi powering down the far wing. He tricked a defender to win himself time and crossed the ball into the six-yard box. Anthony Owusu leapt up to head the ball.

Danny was on his feet before it hit the back

of the net. He knew it was a goal. No question. He shouted, unable to control himself, 'YEEEE-AAAAAAAAHHHHHHHHHHHHHHH!!!!!!'

His celebrations were so loud, several people jumped and Danny felt Holt's hand on his arm.

Holt grimaced. 'Sit down.'

Danny sat down and looked sheepishly around. Some of the Italian journalists were glaring at him.

He put his head down and smiled, listening to the City fans celebrate.

That had shut the racists up, anyway.

'Can we talk, now we're winning?' Danny asked Holt.

'No. Not here. I know it's a huge story. And I believe you. But it's not safe in this stadium. We'll meet tonight. After the game. I'll come to your hotel.'

'OK,' Danny said. But he felt deeply anxious. He wanted to do something about it *now*.

The remainder of the first half did not go so well.

The Forza crowd had been getting more and more unpleasant. More racism aimed at City's black players. More whistling at their own team. It was a very different atmosphere from games in England.

After twenty-seven minutes two Forza players

went down in the City area following a corner kick. The referee pointed to the spot.

'Never a penalty!' Danny shouted, glancing up to see one of the Italian journalists gesturing to him.

Holt kept quiet.

Moments later, Sam Roberts stepped up and scored the penalty for Forza.

1–1.

The crowd went wild, bouncing up and down, twirling their scarves above their heads.

Danny refused to look up at the Italians.

'That was never a penalty,' he said to Holt.

'I know,' Holt muttered.

Then Danny remembered something. 'Do people still bribe referees?'

'Yes,' Holt said. 'But I doubt it would happen in a match this big.'

'Didn't it happen in a European final once?' Danny was remembering the contents of Fo's desk.

'Yes. Leeds–Milan,' Holt said. 'Leeds were cheated out of *two* European trophies. The referee even admitted it.'

Danny scowled.

A few minutes before half-time things got even worse.

Sam Roberts was dominating the game now, like he used to for City. As play moved into first half injury time, he hammered the ball at the goal from thirty yards. A speculative shot. It smashed off the bar and – in Danny's judgement – bounced off the line and into the City keeper's arms.

No goal.

Danny watched Roberts' reaction. He had accepted it hadn't gone in, and had turned to track back up field.

But then Danny heard the roar. The roar of the Forza fans celebrating because the referee had pointed to the centre spot for a restart, meaning he'd given a goal.

Danny stared at the pitch. Then at the giant TV screen above the stand opposite. They were showing the action replay. He watched as it screamed over the City keeper and bounced down off the bar. Then he saw it bounce *on* the line and come back into play.

'No goal!' Danny shouted.

Then he looked up to see several Italian journalists waving pieces of paper at him, cheering.

He fixed his eyes back on the screen. But the footage of the goal-that-wasn't had been replaced now. By a giant image of Salvatore Fo, who was wearing the same smug grin he'd worn at City FC when Kofi had scored his own goal.

Danny felt sick. It was 2–1 to Forza. 3–2 on aggregate. City were losing and going out of the Champions League.

As the match went on, his mind went back to the corridors at school. Seeing Theo Gibbs laughing. And all the other so-called Forza fans. And for some reason, in this hideous anti-fantasy, he could see Charlotte too. Standing with Theo. Had Theo been telling the truth? Was he really going out with Charlotte? And why did that bother Danny so much?

Then there was Fo. Danny had met a lot of dodgy people in football. But Fo was the worst. And he was getting away with murder. The murder of football.

Danny felt a wave of anger sweeping through him like he'd never felt before.

This was too much.

If City lost this, he wasn't sure if he could handle it.

SECOND HALF

Half-time was difficult.

All the journalists came out of the padded blue seating area of the stadium, up a short staircase and into a large room. At one end of the room there was a bar, where journalists were stood talking and drinking espresso.

Danny followed Holt to the bar. He got several smirks and a couple of pats on the back from Italians. They were rubbing it in: Forza were beating City. And all Danny could feel was a deep sense of injustice. There was no way Forza should be 2–1 up. Both their goals had been dodgy.

When he was standing with Holt – and Holt's two friends who wrote about football in other newspapers – Danny couldn't stop himself.

'There's something dodgy about this game,' he seethed.

Holt grinned at his friends. 'Danny sees conspiracy everywhere.'

Danny felt even more angry now. What did Holt mean by that?

'*Was* it a penalty?' he said. '*Did* that ball cross the line for Roberts' goal?'

'That's football, Danny,' Holt said, shooting him a warning look.

He thinks I'm going to talk about Fo, Danny thought. And he felt like it. He hated the way Holt was making him wait before they sorted that out.

'That's how it is in Italy,' the younger of the two other journalists cut in. 'You come to a country like Italy or Spain and the atmosphere forces the referee to make decisions in favour of the home team. It's the same when there's a game in front of a big crowd in England.'

'It doesn't make it fair,' Danny said. 'I think Fo –'

'Do you want another drink, Danny?' Holt grabbed Danny's coffee and started to lead him over to the bar. Once they were away from the others, he spoke again.

'Keep that under your hat, Danny!'

'Why?'

'Why?' Holt asked. 'Because one, we need to

corroborate all the facts you've found out – or we'll end up in an Italian prison. And two, we're in Fo's stadium now and we have to be careful – God knows what could happen.'

Danny folded his arms and frowned.

'You're behaving like a kid, Danny,' Holt said. 'You need to think more.'

Danny looked at Holt again. 'I am a kid,' he said.

The second half did not start well. Forza were going for the jugular.

They attacked in wave after wave. Danny thought it was just a matter of time before they scored again – and silenced the City fans, who were still singing as loudly as the 70,000 Italians.

But with just ten minutes to go, something changed.

The Italian fans were becoming gradually quieter now. And the Italian journalists around Danny were looking fidgety. A sense of nervousness was passing through the stadium like a Mexican wave.

And Danny knew why: there'd been a psychological shift.

Instead of Forza needing one goal to put the result beyond City, City only needed one goal to draw level and win on away goals. Forza would not have time to reply in the few minutes that were left.

And Danny couldn't stop himself. 'COME ON CITY! COME OOOOOOOOOOOOOOOOON!'

For the second time in the match, several Italian journalists jumped. Danny noticed a few of them scowling at him, and some still grinning, as Holt dragged him into his seat.

But Danny was glad of it. He hated their smugness.

With *three* minutes to go, City attacked. Danny looked at the clock. He knew this would be their last – or second last – attack. Kofi got the ball thirty yards out. Forza were stretched, the keeper off his line.

Kofi shot.

The ball dipped as it headed to the goal. And Danny stood up.

'Come OOOOOOOOOONNNN!' he shouted.

But the ball went straight into the keeper's arms, to the sound of more racist chanting at a raised volume from the Forza fans. They knew they were minutes away from the Champions League final.

Danny sat back down to feel a tap on his shoulder.

'Go back to play in England,' an Italian voice said behind him. 'Leave Europe to the important teams.'

Danny didn't even look round.

And it was a good thing he didn't. Because, when the Forza keeper had thrown the ball out, Kofi had sprinted back to challenge the defender who was in possession. Just to put pressure on him, in case he made a mistake.

And it worked!

The defender mis-hit the ball, leaving Kofi in control with only one other defender to beat.

The Forza fans went eerily quiet and all Danny could hear now was the City fans roaring.

This was it: the point in the game where everything could change – or might just stay the same.

Danny watched as Kofi used all his amazing pace to draw the defender to the right of the penalty area. Then the Ghanaian turned and suddenly was one-on-one with the keeper.

The keeper ran ten yards off his line and stood tall to put Kofi off.

He's expecting a chip, Danny thought.

Kofi made as if to chip the ball over the keeper.

The keeper leapt up.

And Danny watched Kofi roll the ball underneath

the keeper, who was trying to turn in midair to do something about stopping it.

But it was too late.

The ball was in the back of the net.

The noise from the City fans was pouring down from the top tiers like a waterfall.

And Danny was on his feet shouting, 'GOOO-OOOOOAAAAAAAAAAAALLLLLL!'

To their credit, many of the Italian journalists came over to Danny after the game and shook his hand.

Danny was moved by that. He doubted he'd have been so nice about it if City had gone out.

'I'll take you up to the players' lounge,' Holt said, in that quick voice he used when he was on a deadline to file his copy, write his match report and email it back to England. 'Then I need to get back down here.'

They walked in silence into the stand, then up a flight of steps.

Halfway up, Holt stopped Danny. They were alone, briefly.

'Don't do anything or say anything,' he said. 'Once I've filed, once we're back in your hotel, we'll sort this out. The Fo stuff. OK?'

Danny shrugged.

'I know you want to nail him,' Holt insisted. 'But we need to be sure of our facts.'

'I am,' Danny said.

'Well, I'm not,' Holt replied.

'I'll see you up here in . . .'

'Less than an hour,' Holt said.

Danny nodded, walked up the remaining steps, showed his pass to the man on the door, then entered the players' lounge. At the invitation of Sam Roberts.

FO

Danny stood on his own for the first few minutes. There were no footballers in the players' lounge yet, just a load of old men in suits and women in posh dresses. Several people had looked over at Danny. *They must think I'm the son of a player or something*, he thought.

He was happy to be on his own, though. He was still buzzing from the win. Now City were in the final of the Champions League. It was beyond his dreams for a football team like City to reach such heights.

After a while several waiters and waitresses arrived with food on trays. Danny knew there was a word for food served like this, but he could never remember it. He also knew that this meant lots more guests would be about to come into the room. This was a well-run operation and he knew the food's arrival would have been timed perfectly.

And then he felt a tap on his shoulder.

Danny turned, expecting to see Anton Holt.

But it wasn't. It was Sam Roberts.

'Hello, Danny. Good mood?'

Danny grinned. 'Hard luck,' he said sheepishly, not sure what to say to a player who has just been robbed of a place in the Champions League final.

Roberts lowered his voice. 'I think City had the hard luck. That was never a goal.'

'No,' Danny said, agreeing.

'Still, I reckon our big boss will be fuming about the result.'

'The manager?'

'No, Mr Fo,' Roberts said, still talking quietly.

Danny said nothing. Although he was bursting to tell Sam Roberts everything. Any mention of that man's name made his hairs stand on end.

'What's he like?' Danny asked, tentatively.

'Mr Fo?' Sam asked.

'Yeah.'

Roberts paused to think. Danny took the time to check there was no one else nearby. Most of the other Forza players were in another corner of the room. There was nobody who could overhear them speaking.

'He's a friendly guy,' Roberts said. 'Chatty.

Generous. A good host of a party ...' Roberts' voice tailed off.

'But?' Danny asked, sensing Roberts had more to say.

'But I wouldn't want to get on his wrong side. Or anyone else's wrong side around here. He ... he reminds me a bit of you-know-who.'

'Who?'

'Our old friend from City.'

'Sir Richard?' Danny asked.

'Yes.'

'Why don't you come back to City?' Danny suggested. 'Sir Richard is long gone.'

And he was surprised by Roberts' response. He had said it as a joke, but Roberts looked genuinely sad.

'I would,' he said quietly. 'There's something ...'

'What?' Danny pressed.

'Nothing,' Roberts said.

That was when Danny decided to take a risk. He knew he could trust Roberts. The player owed him for saving his life and had made it clear he wanted to repay that debt. And Roberts seemed to have a lot to say about Fo. Maybe he could help. Maybe he would *want* to help. Even though Danny knew that Anton would disapprove.

'Look at this,' Danny said. He took out his

iPhone and showed Roberts the image he had found in Fo's desk. 'Does it look familiar?'

He had to pause for a moment as someone came over to talk to Roberts. But Danny was pleased that Roberts seemed to be trying to get rid of them quickly.

He took the time to check a text he'd had from Charlotte.

279 replies from the UK. 134 have satellite. And, this is weird, Danny, 123 of them support Forza. Out of the 145 who don't have satellite, 5 support Forza. Love C x

Danny looked at the figures again and again. This proved it. People with satellite were hundreds times more likely to support Forza. Danny had seen the subliminal images on satellite. That meant that satellite TV was being used to brainwash people into supporting Forza.

When he had his attention again, Danny showed Roberts his phone again.

'Maybe I do recognize it,' Roberts said, putting his head to one side. 'What is it?'

'I think Fo is secretly using this message around the world to make everyone stop supporting their *local* teams, so that they follow

Forza. I paused my TV at home and it came up.'

Roberts nodded. And Danny realized he'd gone too far. He must sound like a madman to Sam Roberts, making up crazy stories.

Then Roberts spoke, still quiet. 'There's more,' he said.

'What?' Danny asked. Was Roberts about to give him some information?

'More stuff like this,' Roberts went on, pointing at Danny's phone, which was still showing the image. 'Things I've seen around the place.'

Suddenly there was a loud noise.

Danny and Roberts turned to see a group of men enter. The City squad. And Kofi was coming in first. The noise was the applause for him.

'You're mates with Danquah, aren't you?' Roberts asked loudly above the clapping.

'Yeah. I've been to Ghana with him,' Danny said, loudly too, putting his iPhone down on the table at his side so he could join in the clapping.

'I'm going over to talk to some of the lads,' Roberts went on. 'Are you coming?'

Danny shook his head. 'I'll wait until it's a bit quieter for Kofi, then go and have a word.' He felt shy of just going over and talking to the City players. He could talk to Roberts and Kofi, but that was because he knew them.

'OK,' Roberts said. 'But we need to talk about that stuff later. Don't go until we have. I'll talk to you later. Yeah?'

'Can we talk to Anton Holt about it?' Danny asked. 'He might do a story.'

Roberts frowned. 'Can I think about it? Just for a few minutes?'

Danny nodded.

Then he watched Sam Roberts walk over to his old City team-mates. He was received with hugs and slaps on the back.

Kofi caught his eye and waved Danny over.

Danny nodded. He stepped back to pick his iPhone up off the table.

Then he was pushed. Only gently, but pushed all the same.

And a hand moved to grab his iPhone off the table.

Danny turned to try to work out what was going on.

A waiter was walking quickly through the crowd. *With* Danny's phone.

He'd been robbed! He couldn't believe it.

Danny started to push his way through the crowd of people. Just as he saw the thief going through a door on the far side of the room.

FO'S CRONIES

Danny moved as quickly as he could across the crowded players' lounge. He knew that if he went out of this room he was putting himself in danger. He would be away from the media and from other English people. But what else could he do? His iPhone had the image from Fo's office on it. Without that he had nothing.

Meaning Fo might get away with it.

Meaning his chance to save City FC was gone.

He had no choice.

Danny went through the door the waiter had disappeared through and found himself in a quiet area, made to seem especially quiet after the noise of the players' lounge. Straight ahead, there was a long corridor. To his left, a staircase down. To his right, a staircase up.

At first Danny felt like chasing after the thief, shouting. But he knew that would be a mistake.

So, even though someone was getting away from him with all the evidence, Danny stopped dead.

Then he listened.

He had got this trick from a crime story he had read to his dad. A detective who, rather than run around shooting, or arriving in noisy cars, would arrive in places on foot, very slowly, very quietly, so that he could listen.

And, over the beating of his heart, Danny heard footsteps descending a staircase.

It was unmistakable. The rhythm of the footsteps. Faster. Heavier. Definitely someone going *down* the stairs rather than up.

Now Danny was running.

He hammered down the stairs as fast as he could. A tight corridor. No pictures on the walls. He wanted his phone. He wanted that image.

When he hit the bottom step he looked to his right and to his left. It was a white corridor with portraits of footballers painted on to the walls. There was a murmur of voices down here. Not the silence of the floor above.

Then Danny saw the waiter. Disappearing into a room at the right end of the corridor, the flash of Danny's iPhone unmistakable in his hand.

Danny was just about to go after him, when the murmur of voices he had heard exploded into the corridor. Another door had opened and a group of men and women were moving towards him, filling the width of the corridor. Danny moved backwards and up on to the bottom step to get out of their way.

He had no choice. He had to delay and let the group pass.

They were all in suits.

All carrying files or papers.

All talking at once in fast Italian.

But one man among them was not carrying papers. And he was not talking. But he *was* looking straight at Danny. And his face was like thunder.

Salvatore Fo.

Fo scowled at Danny, but carried on walking. Danny knew why. He was with other people. He could not be seen to be having an argument with a fifteen-year-old boy. He would leave that to someone else.

But Danny knew that he would be feeling bad about losing. Really bad.

So Danny smiled at him. A mock smile that he knew the Italian would interpret as *We won, you lost*.

Danny stood and watched and did nothing. The two people at the front of the group each opened one of the double doors ahead. The rest of the group – Fo included – moved through them.

As the doors closed Danny saw a sign in two languages: LA SALA DELLA CONFERENZA STAMPA in Italian, PRESS CONFERENCE ROOM in English.

Once the group had passed, Danny jogged to the door at the right end of the corridor.

That was weird. The man he was trying to bring down had just walked past him, seen him and done nothing. And neither had Danny.

But Danny knew Fo would have someone else coming after him. He was the kind of man who never did his own dirty work. And Danny was pretty sure the Italian's expression had meant something too. Something to do with his iPhone and the picture he needed.

Danny walked past the images of players. They were all greats of the Italian game: Paolo Rossi, Paolo Maldini, Francesco Totti, John Charles.

But he didn't have time to congratulate himself about footballers he could identify. He had to get his phone back. And he had already lost a lot of time.

He gently pushed the door the waiter had gone through.

There was no light on. But the floodlighting from the stadium outside illuminated what Danny could see was a small room. Like a hospitality box that looked out on to the pitch.

Danny stepped in, fumbling for a light switch.

When it came on he was alone.

Had he got the wrong room?

Had the waiter gone through another door and made his escape?

Was there a way out into the stands?

Damn it! he thought. He'd lost the waiter. *And* lost the phone.

Then he felt a sharp jab in his back.

He didn't react by moving. There was no point. He knew what this was.

He was being held.

At gunpoint.

No question.

A voice said, '*Andiamo!*'

Danny moved into the room. He knew what was meant. *Move! Let's go!*

In the reflection of the glass through which Danny could see the stadium, lights flickering out, empty now of fans and stewards, Danny saw who had him at gunpoint.

Not Salvatore Fo.

It was the waiter.

And Danny knew he'd been lured into a trap.

CERTAIN DEATH

Danny knew he was in big trouble.

As the waiter had come up behind him, having tricked him into the room first, this, Danny thought again, was *clearly* a trap. And because it was a trap that made things worse than just being caught. If someone *went out of their way* to capture you, it meant they probably had plans for you. And not nice plans.

Danny walked across the room, watching the waiter's reflection in the window. They were in a hospitality box, its glass front looking out into the stadium. But Danny could not see beyond the reflection now. The stadium and all its trappings meant nothing. He knew he had to wait for instructions. And they came quickly.

'Sit.'

Danny sat, turning to look at his captor.

He was tall and wiry, with black hair and a thin

moustache. He wore a black suit and a white shirt. And, in his hand, he held one of the large semi-automatic machine guns Danny had seen at Fo's villa.

Not good.

The man had said nothing since ordering Danny to sit down. But Danny was feeling anxious. So anxious that he decided to speak. Because he couldn't bear doing nothing: he would rather be running away from this man, climbing the floodlights. Anything but sitting here.

'Why are you holding me here?' he asked.

'I am told to keep you here,' was the short reply.

'By who?'

'You know.'

'Fo?'

The man stared at Danny. But he didn't reply.

'What's he going to do with me?' Danny asked, leaning forward.

The man ran his finger across his throat and grinned. Then he said, 'Wait to see.' And the gunman abruptly cut the lights.

Danny closed his eyes. Now what?

Think.

That was what now was about.

Don't panic. Calm down. Ask yourself questions. First of all, how long did he have?

If Fo had been going into the press room it was likely he was giving a press conference. How long would that take? Fifteen minutes? Maybe less because his team had lost. He might not be in the mood to talk to the media.

So what should Danny do?

How could he escape?

How should he think about this?

Calmly, he told himself again. That was the main thing.

He had read about a trick in another of his dad's crime books. A private investigator had always got out of scrapes by imagining he was someone else. So, if *he* was trapped in a room with a gunman, he would think about how *another* man, just like him, could escape. That way, the investigator had worked out, it felt less desperate, less personal. And therefore calmer.

So, as the gunman stared blankly at him, Danny closed his eyes and thought.

What were the facts?

A boy in a room.

A man with a gun keeping him there.

Someone coming in five or ten minutes who wants to silence – quite possibly kill – the boy.

A window out on to a massive stadium.

No lights on in the room, so no one can see them from outside.

Three large chairs and a medium-sized table. A bar of bottles and glasses.

Two doors to the room. Both doors closed.

Voices in the corridor.

Danny's mind moved into a higher gear.

Voices?

Fo coming to kill him now?

No. They were English voices.

Danny looked around the room again.

What should the boy do?

Make some noise.

When?

Now.

So Danny jumped to his feet, picked up the table with all his strength and threw it at the window.

For a second it looked like the table had just bounced off the glass, but then there was a spectacular crash, as the window burst out into the stadium.

Danny heard the voices outside get louder as he saw his captor turn first to him, then the door.

The gunman was confused, unsure what to do.

That gave Danny another second.

He leapt over to the bar. He wasn't thinking in a detached way now. There was no need. He was in the moment.

As the gunman turned back to Danny, Danny started his assault, throwing bottle after bottle at the man. Bottles of wine. Bottles of lager. Bottles of anything. And because he threw them so quickly, the gunman could do nothing. He couldn't aim his weapon. He couldn't even look up, as he cowered by the main door. And that was what helped Danny.

Two doors.

Danny threw three more bottles at the man, who was bleeding around his neck and face, and then burst through the side door.

He found himself in an exact replica of the hospitality room he'd just come from. Only without the reek of alcohol and the gunman.

He hit the door going out to the corridor and headed back the way he'd come.

He knew, deep down, that his chances of getting out of the stadium without being seen were low, his chances of escaping from Fo almost impossible.

So what now?

Give up?

Never.

He needed to find a way out of this. And the best way to do that was to think about the books he'd read.

When had he read about this kind of scenario in one of his dad's crime thrillers? Several times. And what had *they* done?

He tried to think. He could only remember chases and fights. But he didn't fancy that.

And then it came. Like it always did.

One hero in a crime story – he couldn't remember which one – had been unable to get away from his enemy. So instead of running away he'd got close.

So Danny ran.

Hard.

Up the corridor. Past the group of people speaking English, all of whom had stopped in shock at the noise and chaos Danny had created. Towards the double doors marked PRESS CONFERENCE ROOM, where he could hear a murmur of voices and camera clicks.

And, without a thought, he burst through the doors.

Then he stopped.

Because Danny found himself facing the world's TV, newspaper and radio media. Cameras trained on him. Microphones aimed at him. One hundred faces looking up at him, pausing to take a breath to hear what this boy who had just crashed a major sporting press conference had to say.

His first thought was, *I'm safe.*

His second thought was, *What the hell am I going to say to them?*

LIVE FROM FORZA FC

Danny swallowed hard. He knew he had to speak now – or he'd be dragged away like some football hooligan from a fight.

He was standing on a stage.

To his left was a long table where Salvatore Fo was sitting in front of a large bunch of microphones. Next to Fo were Umberto Calvino, the Forza FC manager, and Sam Roberts. And, on the table, a small marble model of the Forza stadium.

The rest of the room, offstage, was filled with over a hundred seats, all packed with journalists. At the back were dozens of lights and cameras, all clicking. Danny saw everyone swivel towards him. The bright lights were beguiling.

Given the unique opportunity to tell the world about one of the darkest crimes in the history of football, Danny froze.

His mind went blank.

His mouth went dry.

He just stood there.

And, to make it worse, a murmuring was growing in the room. Short snorts of laughter. All aimed at Danny.

And then he heard a voice. A familiar voice.

'Anton Holt. *Evening Post*, England. Is there anything you would like to tell us?'

Danny took a breath. The room had gone quiet again.

'I . . . er . . . I . . . have some information,' Danny stuttered, grateful that his friend had rescued him.

Another silence followed. A silence Danny knew that he had to fill. He steeled himself. No messing about. Just straight to it.

He cleared his throat.

'Salvatore Fo is using subliminal images on TV screens across the world that brainwash people into supporting Forza FC.'

There. He'd said it.

Suddenly the room exploded with laughter. Everyone was looking at the table, at Fo.

Danny looked at him too. He was writing something on a large sheet of paper, a broad grin on his face. Once he had finished, he held it up:

THIS ENGLISH CHILD IS CRAZY.

But then another voice interrupted the mockery. An Italian voice.

'Mona Levi, investigative journalist, Italian Press Agency.'

Danny looked at the woman. She was standing. She had short dark hair and was wearing a silver scarf around her neck. And when she started to speak, the room went deadly quiet.

'Can you tell us what evidence you have for this acc– suggestion?'

Danny looked at her. She was smiling. And he could tell she was a good person. That she wanted to help him.

'I saw a freeze frame saying "Support Forza FC. Your team. Your success" on my TV at home. During the first leg. Then I . . .' Danny wondered if he should admit this. And he remembered his dad's mantra: always the truth. 'Then, when I was looking around Mr Fo's office, I took a photo of a document of the image in his desk.'

There was a gasp and laughter from around the room. And Danny glanced at Fo, who was now glaring at him, and taking notes.

'And he speaks a lot about subliminal art. And he has a huge collection of subliminal art, especially Tomassina Tremezzo. And . . .' Danny knew he was running out of steam. He wanted to be honest. He wanted to get across how angry he was that everyone was supporting some massive football team and not their local ones. 'And in my city suddenly everyone is supporting Forza FC. Even my sister. And there is no explanation for it other than this.' Danny could feel his anger close to the surface now. He felt better. 'Why would they support Forza FC? Not because they are in the Champions League any more!'

The room exploded with laughter again. From both English and Italian journalists.

Danny glanced at Fo, who had his arms folded.

'Yes, I like Tremezzo's work. No, I am not using subliminal messages. I think this boy, who I met with his mother yesterday, is a little cross with me. His mother, I think, found me attractive. And this boy is angry that his parents are to divorce.'

Danny felt his insides crumple, like he had been kicked in the groin.

The room had gone quiet again as journalists wrote notes in their pads. Notes about Danny's mum and dad.

This man was a horrible man.

This man thought he could get to Danny.

And he had.

So now Danny wanted to deal with him more than anything. He had taken on worse people than this. People who used football and its fans to make money and get their own bullying way.

Not this time.

Not here.

Not today.

'You just had me locked in a room with a gunman,' Danny spat. 'He was under orders to kill me.'

Fo shook his head. 'No.'

'You did.'

'Prove it, boy,' Fo said.

Danny was about to ask the hundred or so people to follow him to the room where the gunman had held him, when Fo spoke again.

'And, please, show us the image you have.'

'I can't,' Danny said. 'One of your men has taken my phone.'

He was starting to realize he sounded more and more like a crazy little English boy. Every time Fo asked for evidence, he had none.

Then another voice. Forza's coach, Umberto Calvino. 'Can we get this press conference over with?' he asked. 'I have a lot to do.'

'Yes,' Fo said, agreeing. 'Take the boy outside. And, Mr Calvino, because my team Forza have lost today, you will be taken outside also. You're fired.'

There was a huge gasp. Fo had just sacked Forza's manager in front of the world's media. It was controversial. It was shocking. And now nobody had any thoughts about the English boy with the vague accusations.

Danny stared at the ceiling.

The room was filled with voices so loud the walls seemed to be vibrating. Even if Danny spoke now, no one would hear him.

He *could* see Anton Holt and Mona Levi trying to speak above the noise. But it was useless.

Suddenly Danny's arms were taken – gently – by two uniformed women.

They moved him off the stage, past the marble model of the Forza stadium. And no one was trying to stop them.

It was over.

FOOTBALL SUPERHERO

Just as Danny thought he'd blown it – that his chance to reveal the deepest and darkest of football crimes had gone – another voice came from the table at the front of the press conference.

'Wait.'

Danny looked round. The sound and fury of the room had stopped abruptly.

Sam Roberts was standing, both hands raised. He spoke clearly and slowly, in English. 'I have something to say.'

Danny felt the grip of the two security guards loosen, although they still held him.

It amazed him that a footballer could stop a room like that, even change the behaviour of security guards. But he was glad it had happened. It reminded him of Billy Giles back at the City meeting last week.

'I believe what Danny says,' Roberts declared. 'He is always right about things like this.'

Now the room was filled with noise again. Questions were being fired at Roberts.

'What do you know about the boy?'

'Have you any evidence against Mr Fo?'

'What other things are you talking about?'

Question after question after question.

Still Roberts stood with his arms raised. Next to him Fo sat like an animal calculating its next move, his eyes flitting from Danny to Roberts to the crowds of journalists.

When the room was quiet again, Roberts spoke.

'As you know, a year ago I was kidnapped. My kidnapper was Sir Richard Gawthorpe. At the time, two local men in England were reported to be the ones who rescued me. But that wasn't true.'

Danny watched the room taking notes, holding microphones in Roberts' direction. The player had never spoken about his ordeal, even when he was offered a million pounds to sell his story, so this was a major coup for the media.

'The reason I was rescued and the reason that Sir Richard was exposed as my kidnapper was because of this boy.'

Again, a barrage of questions.

'How could a child rescue you?'

'Are you just making this up to rescue *him*?'

'What has this got to do with Mr Fo?'

Again, Roberts held his hands up until there was silence.

'Danny Harte must be listened to. I know for a fact that, as well as saving me, he has helped other England and City FC players with various problems. It is not for me to say what they are, but Danny is a sort of football superhero. When he turns up you know there's something that needs sorting out. And I do not want to see him taken into the custody of anyone until this *is* sorted out.'

'What cases?'

'What other players?'

Roberts paused before answering. He looked at Danny, as if he was asking for permission to speak.

Danny nodded and felt the arms of his captors release him. Both women smiled and brushed down his clothes where they had been holding him, as if in apology.

'Three England players,' Roberts declared, 'who were being blackmailed and intimidated by a Russian billionaire. A young African footballer whose agent was cheating him. Several City FC players who were being burgled.'

Danny watched Roberts closely, wondering how he knew all this. He glanced back at Anton Holt who smiled sheepishly as he made his way through the crowded room towards Danny.

'Mr Fo was handed an iPhone by a waiter a few minutes ago,' Holt said, interrupting. 'One that had a City FC sticker on the back. I expect that's your phone, Danny?'

Danny nodded. The waiter must have sneaked on to the stage when Danny was being moved off it. 'It has the image on it,' he said.

As he spoke, another commotion started. A chair had been kicked back against the wall and Salvatore Fo was on his feet. He turned quickly and made for a door at the side of the room, the iPhone in his hand.

'Stop him!' shouted Mona Levi, the journalist. 'He mustn't get away.'

And Danny found that he was holding the marble model of the football stadium in his hand. Instinct had taken over as he lifted it and, doing his best to be accurate, hurled it over Sam Roberts and his confused club coach.

The room watched as one as the model arced over the stage towards Fo. And cheered as it hit him on the back just as he reached the door.

The Italian stumbled, then collapsed. And the two security guards moved towards him, to help him to his feet.

PART THREE: ENGLAND

THURSDAY

FAME

Danny had two things to worry about when he arrived back in England.

The first was his mum. She had started talking at him the moment they were sat down, in standard class, on the flight home.

When they'd got on to the plane, the captain had come out and offered to upgrade them to first-class seats. Because Danny was a hero. But Mum said no: she didn't want her son being rewarded for putting his life at risk.

As they sat down and fastened their safety belts, Mum whispered, 'This is the last time, Danny.'

Danny did not answer.

He knew she was angry. And, even though he had stopped a major crime being committed and saved City FC from who knew what, she was still his mum.

'I said so before,' she persisted. 'I will not have you putting your life in danger like this.'

Danny had told her about the chase, being caught and the gunman in the stadium. He felt he owed her the absolute truth after the events of the night before, which she had first been aware of in the hotel bar, when she saw his face on the TV screen.

'Look at me, Danny.'

Danny looked at his mum. He knew she was going to make him promise. Promise to give up his football detecting. He wasn't stupid.

The only thing was, he *felt* stupid. Because he had no idea what he should say to answer her.

So on she went.

'I know your dad lets you get involved in these kinds of things, but I will *not*,' she said. 'I think he is wrong. I think he is being a bad parent letting you put your life at risk. And, frankly, that difference of opinion between him and me is one of the reasons we are splitting up.' She looked sad, her eyes reddening.

Danny looked down at his hands. He knew that already. He felt tears forming in his eyes. They were going back to that. Back to arguments. Back to a cold atmosphere in the family home. Back to him and his mum and his dad at war.

Danny looked up at his mum. 'What if I stop? If I promise to stop everything?'

Danny's mum looked at him strangely. She had heard his voice wobbling. She put her hand on his, speaking in a soft voice now, the kind of voice she used to use with him when he was younger, before all this.

'It won't make a difference, Danny,' she said. 'Your dad and I . . . we . . . we've grown apart.'

'You just said it was my fault,' Danny said. 'So if I stop –'

'No,' Mum interrupted. 'That was wrong of me. It's not your fault. It's mine.' Now *her* voice was wobbling.

Danny felt that heavy sensation in his stomach again. Something he couldn't put into words. A bad feeling. As bad as anything he had ever felt before. Or worse.

And that was when the engines fired and the plane raced down the runway.

On the flight, Danny read the day's English newspapers.

He was on the cover of most of them. BOY BRINGS DOWN OLD FO. Stuff like that.

According to the newspapers, the Italian female journalist who had been in the press conference had added dozens of other crimes to Fo's charge sheet. They predicted he would live the rest of his life in prison.

There was good news on the back pages too.

City FC were through to the Champions League final. He knew that. He had been there. But he still read the match report three times.

And, as a result of the confusion around City's ownership and the main interested party pulling out, the fans were going to be offered the chance to own the club, according to the club's administrators.

Danny grinned. This could not get much better.

The second thing Danny had to worry about was the number of TV cameras and microphones pointing at him in the airport when he arrived back in England.

As they came into Arrivals, he noticed people pointing and taking his photo.

Then all hell was let loose. Camera flashes. Shouts.

'Danny! Tell us how you took on Fo. Were you scared?'

'Danny! You've saved City FC. Do you want to be the new chairman?'

'Can you tell us about all the football crimes you've solved?'

'Have you been offered a book deal?'

'Can we have a photo of you wearing this?' another asked, throwing a City FC scarf at him.

The questions just confused Danny. He had often wondered what it would be like to be famous. So far, it didn't feel that good. Especially following the conversation with his mum. All he wanted to do was get away.

They tried to get out of the arrivals area, but were mobbed by journalists and people taking photos. It was hopeless. Soon they were backed up against a wall, next to a door.

'Do you see what I mean?' Mum asked. 'This is not good.'

'No,' Danny said, as he saw a group of security people move towards them.

'I want a promise from you. Now,' Mum said quietly.

Danny looked at her. She was not being angry or bossy. She seemed more scared than anything. And Danny felt a powerful wave of guilt. For what he'd put his mum through.

'You *will* be killed,' she went on. 'You're not James Bond. You're not Superman. You're not one of the heroes of one of your dad's crime thrillers. You're a fifteen-year-old boy who is lucky to be alive . . .'

Danny swallowed. 'OK,' he said.

'. . . and if you want to join the police when you are eighteen, then I will back you all the way. I'd be proud of you.' Mum's voice broke again. 'I am proud of you . . . but . . .'

'OK,' Danny said again. 'I'll stop.'

And he meant it.

FRIDAY

HERO

Danny stood on the stage in the school hall and tried to pick out Charlotte from among the faces in the crowd.

It was the only way he could cope with the applause and – it was hard to believe – screaming that was coming from the 1,500 children in front of him.

He did not like this. He did not want this. But the headteacher had insisted.

'As we have all seen on our television screens last night, and in the newspapers today,' the Head said, 'we have a hero in our school.'

More applause. More screaming. Girls waving to Danny from the crowd to catch his eye. But none of them was Charlotte.

Where *was* she?

'Danny has done this city – and the world – a great service,' the Head went on.

Danny tried to smile, to look grateful. But all he felt was embarrassed. He had never done what he did for fame or applause. He did it for football.

'However,' the Head said. 'It stops here.'

The hall went quiet.

'From now on Danny is Danny again. From now on he is just another boy at this school. A boy who should be taking his GCSEs a bit more seriously. A boy who will not be taking on all manner of megalomaniacs around the world.'

Danny looked at the headteacher and nodded. He wanted the Head to know that he agreed with what he was saying. Wholeheartedly.

And then his eyes fell on Charlotte. She smiled up at him. A big, beaming, brilliant smile. Danny smiled too. Until he saw an arm snaked around the back of Charlotte's chair. And saw whose arm it was.

Theo Gibbs. Staring up at him, cocky as ever.

After assembly, Danny was told to go back to class.

He walked the long corridor from the hall, towards the stairs. And there, hanging around the sixth form entrance, was Theo Gibbs. Two mates with him, as usual.

Gibbs started without hesitating. 'I've been looking after Charlotte while you've been away,' he said, smirking.

Danny said nothing, just kept walking.

'I said –'

'I heard you,' Danny snapped back. 'Did you enjoy the *match*?'

'Football?' Gibbs sneered. 'That's for kids.'

'You're right,' Danny answered. 'Maybe that's why I like it so much.'

'And maybe,' Theo said, 'that's why I'm seeing Charlotte and you're not.'

Danny knew there was nothing you could do about people like Theo Gibbs. You had to let them wash over you. You had to try not to get caught up in their weird confrontational logic.

So he walked off.

To silence.

Maybe Theo had been expecting him to try to hit him.

After English, Danny walked the back way, to avoid seeing anyone. Then he slipped down the staircase at the far end of school, down to the bottom flight, that nobody used, where he used to meet Charlotte.

He wanted to be alone.

He wanted not to be hassled by people who thought he was famous.

He just wanted to be Danny Harte, City FC fan.

He sat alone for the first five minutes of break, not really thinking. Just gazing out of the window.

Then he heard footsteps coming down the stairs.

And he did what he always did. Sat still. Made no noise.

People never came down here.

Until today.

The footsteps became louder. But, although his heart had started beating faster, Danny was not worried. He knew whose footsteps they were.

He looked up.

Charlotte.

'Hey,' he said.

'Hey, Mr Bigshot.'

'You OK?'

'Yeah, listen . . . Danny . . .'

This was it. Charlotte's voice had gone serious.

'I'm listening,' Danny said.

'Theo Gibbs has been telling everyone that me and him are going out together now.'

'I know,' Danny said.

'And what do you think of that?' Charlotte asked.

'If it's true and if you're happy then I'm happy,' Danny said, weakly.

'That's not the response I was looking for,' Charlotte replied, a cold tone to her voice.

'No?'

'No.'

'In that case,' Danny said, feeling an energy beneath his feet like something underground was going to come up and carry him off, 'I hate it. I hate Theo Gibbs and I . . . don't hate you.'

Charlotte sat down.

'That's more like it,' she said.

And Danny knew instantly that he had been an idiot to think his best friend was going out with his worst enemy.

Walking home that day, after school, Danny went through the park, passing the house where Sir Richard Gawthorpe used to live.

He remembered when Sir Richard Gawthorpe was his worst enemy. That was where all this had started.

His time as a football detective had been exciting.

But Danny had made a promise to his mum and he was going to keep it.

And when he was eighteen, he would join the

police and work his way up to being a detective, so he could be like the characters in the books he had read to his dad. Men who solved crimes by finding things out, turning them over in their minds, then going to places to find more things out.

A bit like the authors who write books, he thought.

Then, once he was an experienced detective, he would specialize in football crime and take on the next generation of people who thought football was about making money at any cost.

That was his ambition now.

Because *he* knew what football was really about.

THANK-YOUS

Thank you to my wife and daughter. Without their support and love these books would never get written. This book was particularly special because they came with me on my research trip this time. You'll find my daughter in an Italian gift shop about halfway through the novel.

Thank you too to the Bear Cafe in Todmorden, where I wrote most of the book during the summer of 2010. If you are ever passing through Todmorden, the Bear is opposite the public library in the centre. They do very nice cakes.

Thank you to the library, too, for getting me the books I needed to create Salvatore Fo and for feeding my family with great reading material.

Several people read this book and helped me improve it. They were my wife Rebecca, Sophie Hannah, Dan Jones, James Nash and David Luxton. Thank you for your help!

David is my agent. He does lots of things to make me able to 'live my dream' of being an author. Without him none of this would have been possible. I thank him for that and apologize for using the phrase 'living the dream', which is a double-edged sword for Leeds fans like he and I.

And thank you to Ghyllgrove Junior School who test read all my books and where I am proud to say I have been an adopted author for three years.

Thank you finally to everyone at Puffin, who do so much to get the books out there, looking so good – Alex Antscherl, Lindsey Heaven, Wendy Tse, Vanessa Godden and Lisa Hayden, to name just a few. I am, as ever, thrilled to be published by Puffin and am very grateful for all you do.

This book is dedicated to my sister, Sarah. I based Danny's sister, Emily, on Sarah. In the early books in this series Emily is a bit more of a handful than Sarah was to me, but Emily matures into a wonderful sibling for Danny, just like Sarah has for me.

TOM PALMER Q&A

Danny gets to travel abroad to watch his team in *Own Goal*. Have you ever done that?

Yes, I have been to watch Leeds play in France, Belgium, Holland and Spain. Spain was the best: it was at Real Madrid.

Do you think some football-club owners are too powerful, like Fo in the story?

Some football-club owners are good, but others are not. I think the ones who consider the fans are the best. I have read about some maniac football-club owners abroad who have done all of the things covered in the Foul Play series. Almost.

Have there been any real-life uses of subliminal advertising?

Yes. In the 1950s companies used to flash up their products on TV screens. But it was made illegal because it gave everyone the urge to buy things that they maybe didn't want.

Which country have you most enjoyed visiting for book research?

Italy, actually. Because it is beautiful and they do good chocolate, wine, coffee, pizza and football.

As this is the last book in the Foul Play sequence, what are you going to write next?

A new series called The Squad, out in May 2012. It's about an English youth football team who go abroad to play games, but half of them also spy on behalf of the government.

Ten REAL football crimes

1. In the mid-1990s several English Premiership evening games had to be postponed mid-game because betting syndicates tampered with the floodlights, switching the lights off.

2. In 1966 the World Cup trophy was stolen from a window in Birmingham, where it was being displayed to promote the World Cup finals. It was found later by a dog.

3. Several Liverpool players have been burgled in the last few years while they played away in Europe. Most notably, Steven Gerrard's wife was confronted by four masked men in 2007.

4. Former Everton and West Ham star Mark Ward was jailed for renting a house that was used to store £1 million's worth of illegal drugs.

5. In 2007 a friend of German football supremo Franz Beckenbauer was shot dead in South Africa as the country prepared for the World Cup preliminary draw. On the same day the German team manager had his briefcase stolen.

6. In 2007 Newcastle midfielder Joey Barton was jailed for 74 days for having a fight outside a Liverpool nightclub.

7. In 1994 the Columbian defender Andres Escobar was shot dead, following his scoring of a notorious own goal in the 1994 World Cup finals. Many think it was because drug barons lost a lot of money because of the goal.

8. In 2008 another Colombian player shot dead a fan who'd heckled him about how badly he had been playing. He was jailed.

9. In 1970 Bobby Moore, the England captain, was arrested in Colombia and charged with stealing jewellery. He was quickly released, once it became clear he had been set up.

10. In 2007 the former Manchester City keeper Ashley Timms admitted to trying to blackmail a Premier League footballer, claiming he had an interesting video of him.

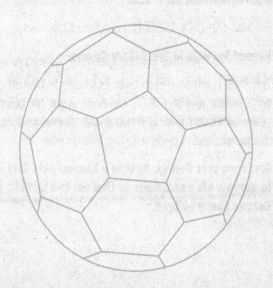

Ten things you (possibly) didn't know about TOM PALMER

Tom was possibly left as newborn in a box at the door of an adoption home in 1967.

He has got an adopted dad and a step-dad, but has never met his real dad.

Tom's best job – before being an author – was a milkman. He delivered milk for nine years.

He once scored two goals direct from the corner flag in the same game. It was very windy.

Tom did not read a book by himself until he was seventeen.

In 1990 Tom wrecked his knee while playing for Bulmershe College in Reading. He didn't warm up and has regretted it ever since.

He was the UK's 1997 Bookseller of the Year.

He met his wife in the Sahara Desert.

Tom has been to watch over 500 Leeds United games, with Leeds winning 307. He once went for twenty-one years without missing a home game. His wife has been ten times, with Leeds winning every time.

Tom once met George Best in a London pub. Tom wanted to borrow his newspaper to find out the football scores. George kindly obliged.

It all started with a Scarecrow.

Puffin is seventy years old.
Sounds ancient, doesn't it? But Puffin has never been
so lively. We're always on the lookout for the next big
idea, which is how it began all those years ago.

Penguin Books was a big idea from the mind of
a man called Allen Lane, who in 1935 invented
the quality paperback and changed the world.
**And from great Penguins, great Puffins grew,
changing the face of children's books forever.**

The first four Puffin Picture Books were hatched in 1940 and the
first Puffin story book featured a man with broomstick arms called
Worzel Gummidge. In 1967 Kaye Webb, Puffin Editor, started the
Puffin Club, promising to **'make children into readers'**.
She kept that promise and over 200,000 children became
devoted Puffineers through their quarterly instalments of
Puffin Post, which is now back for a new generation.

Many years from now, we hope you'll look back and
remember Puffin with a smile. **No matter what your age
or what you're into, there's a Puffin for everyone.**
The possibilities are endless, but one thing is for sure:
whether it's a picture book or a paperback, a sticker book
or a hardback, **if it's got that little Puffin
on it – it's bound to be good.**